Winter Festival Murder
Linnea West

Winter Festival Murder

Copyright © 2018 Linnea West

All rights reserved.

Winter Festival Murder

•Chapter One•

January in Shady Lake, Minnesota can usually be described as really, really cold. It seems that there is always at least a week's stretch or maybe even longer where the high temperature of the day doesn't even get above zero. But when you move to Minnesota, that is kind of what you sign up for.

I don't mind the cold as long as there is snow. Every once in a while, there is a cold spell where it is below zero for days without any snow in sight or even on the ground. It is a miserable feeling to be able to see your breath but the streets are just dirty and icy.

One bright spot in our winter now is the Below Zero Festival that Shady Lake has been throwing for the past five years. The town council got together and decided they needed a bright spot in the middle of winter. After the holidays in December, winter can drag on for a long, long time. (There was even a year that it snowed two feet in May and there was a snow day just a few weeks before school let out for the summer.)

The Below Zero Festival had any sort of winter activity you can imagine involved in it. There is a week-long medallion hunt, snowshoe hikes, sledding parties, a dance, an outdoor hockey game, ice skating on the lake, an ice fishing competition, and many more things. It gets people out of the house and moving around and hopefully, happy enough to stick it out through the rest of winter. Maybe not the rest of winter, but people would at least be able to make it to spring break when they could fly somewhere warm for another break.

The entire town was decorated for it. Everyone left their outdoor holiday decorations up and lit them up again like it was December again. The entire downtown still had large garlands and lights up, but the wreaths had been replaced by large snowflakes. The festival gave us another chance to use the beautiful decorations that had been put up in December.

This is actually the first time I'll be able to go to the Below Zero Festival as I just moved back to Shady Lake this year. After I moved away and went to college, I moved to the Twin Cities with my husband Peter. I had been living the high life until Peter died in a car accident and I had gone into a tailspin. My parents had thankfully recognized that and came up to collect me and bundle me off home here to Shady Lake.

So now I am a thirty year old woman who lives with her parents, but that is alright because my parents actually live in a bed and breakfast so I feel like that makes it less weird. I have five siblings so we lived in a larger home as we were growing up. Instead of selling the house and downsizing when most of us moved out, they built on an addition to live in and made our house into a bed and breakfast.

Tonight is the kickoff for the festival. The entire length of downtown was blocked off as a sort of street party. I pulled my station wagon into the public parking lot downtown and shut it off. Townspeople were already milling about everywhere even though it wasn't actually supposed to start for another half hour or so. Everyone was bundled up in big puffy jackets, knit hats with pom-poms and big warm mittens. I couldn't tell who anyone was, but I was sure I knew most of them. Shady Lake is a smaller town that feels a lot smaller than what the population sign says. I'd have to wait until I was closer to tell who anyone was.

Businesses had sales sitting out on folding tables on the sidewalk, selling things like mittens and hot chocolate. My best friend Mandy runs the Donut Hut and even though it usually closed at lunchtime, Mandy had made a bunch of extra donuts to sell at the kickoff tonight so I decided to go find her table first. One of my major downfalls is that I often let my sweet tooth lead the way.

"I'm off to find Mandy," I said as my parents and I climbed out of the car. "Would you like to come with me?"

Winter Festival Murder

"We will definitely be getting some donuts, but not yet," my mother Teri said as she looked in the mirror and adjusted her hat. "First I'd like to check out some of the sales before all of the good stuff is gone. Sue said she had some cute, locally-made mittens that I'm sure are going to sell out very, very fast."

My father Gary was standing behind her and he rolled his eyes slightly at her mitten excitement, but followed along when she set off in search of the mittens. My parents were the kind of couple that I wanted to find a love like. I'm not quite ready for a serious relationship right now, but I think one day I will find love again.

And speaking of love, Clark Hutchins was headed towards me right now. Clark was a little different from the other men in town because he wasn't actually from Shady Lake. He moved here a few years ago to teach social studies at the high school.

"Hi there Tessa," Clark called. He gave a little wave and a wink as he walked towards me.

Clark was tall and handsome with dark hair and dark eyes. He was literally tall, dark, and handsome. And for some reason, he liked me. I could never quite figure out why. I try to be kind to myself and I am certainly much nicer to myself than I had been as a teenager. But I am short, a bit on the dumpy side, and while I think I have a cute face, I have no idea how to accentuate it with makeup or a cute hairstyle. In short, I have no idea why he has decided to date me, but I'm glad he has. I did have a deep, dark fear that I don't really like him, but just enjoyed the attention from someone I haven't known my entire life. For now, I pushed that fear down and just admired his handsome face.

"Hey Clark," I said as he walked up. He wrapped me in his arms and I pressed my face into his chest. I could feel the warmth coming from him and I would have loved to stay hugging him for a while, but I finally had to let go.

"Mayor Green is going to give his speech soon," Clark said, taking my mitten clad hand in his. "Let's go give it a listen."

I let him lead me towards the small stage that had been set up in the intersection of Main Street and First Avenue. Everyone was slowly making their way over and I waved at people here and there, even though there were several people I couldn't recognize from the thin strip of face showing between their coat collar and their hat. I took the risk of waving to people I didn't know well and all of my waves were well-received because that's just small town living.

•Chapter Two•

Ronald Green, the mayor of Shady Lake, was pacing back and forth on the stage. He wasn't nervous, he was just trying to greet each and every person as they approached the stage for his speech. Ronald was a short, pudgy man with a proclivity for wearing sweater vests. Strangely enough he was called Mayor Panda by most people, but sometimes when you glance at him, you could swear he was a giant panda in a checkered sweater vest.

As I walked up to the stage, I glanced around for Ronald's wife. Melinda was standing towards the side of the stage scowling. Everyone was giving her a wide berth because she was a generally grumpy woman. While Ronald was an ever-cheerful man, Melinda made up for it by never being happy. Somehow she and Ronald went together, happy and grumpy. All of Ronald's love for Shady Lake was balanced out by Melinda's contempt for the town. Even before he was elected mayor, Ronald had insisted on being at every single activity that Shady Lake had to offer. Wherever Ronald went, Melinda went also even though all she did was stand to the side with a frown on her face.

When Ronald spotted me, he gave a big wave. I waved back, eager for the festival week to start.

Winter Festival Murder

When I lived in the big city I had worked in marketing and now that I was back in town, I was putting my skills to the test by marketing all of the activities that Shady Lake had to offer.

Ronald checked his watch and then stepped up to the microphone with a large smile on his face. The crowd quieted down so they could hear our beloved mayor speak.

"Hello everyone," Ronald said. "I'm so glad you all came out for this very cold start to the Below Zero Festival. I'm sure you've all seen the list of activities going on this week and have made a plan to make it out to as many as possible. Let me give you a quick run-down of what this week will have in store for us."

Ronald read down the list of the festival activities and when he got to the snowman building competition, Clark squeezed my hand.

"I think we should enter the snowman competition," Clark whispered to me.

I nodded back to him and hoped I wouldn't get in over my head. I had a bad habit of agreeing to do too much at one time and then becoming overwhelmed. And I really didn't want to let Clark down because I was already unsure of my feelings for him when he was happy with me. Upsetting him would send my emotions into a tailspin. I tried to push that thought out of my head.

"Now I'd like to tell you about what I think is

the most exciting part of the festival," Ronald said. "Every year, Officer Max Marcus hides a gold festival medallion somewhere within the city limits of Shady Lake. In previous years, the prize has been $50. This year, we are so excited to announce that the prize is now $500."

The audience oohed and awed even though this wasn't actually news. The Shady Lake Tribune had announced the new prize last week when they did a large story on the festival.

In fact, their intrepid reporter Chelsea Goodman was standing at the front of the stage, hurriedly scribbling in her notebook. She turned and caught my eye and while I gave her a small wave, she simply narrowed her eyes at me and turned back to the stage. We went to school together and while I'm a bit unclear why, she does not like me. Oh well, I tried to keep rising above and being the bigger person. But not always.

"I'd like to welcome Officer Marcus to the stage to tell us a little bit more about the medallion hunt," Ronald said.

Max stepped up to the microphone and gave me a wink. We had dated for several years in high school and always thought we would get married. But I had moved away to college and we had ended up getting married to different people. Oddly enough, Max's wife had died of cancer just months before Peter had died. I also dated Max, which in contrast with the freshness of my relationship with Clark, had a comforting familiarity. He was also the opposite of Clark in terms of looks too. Max was short and stocky, but in a muscular way. He had blond hair and blue eyes that could melt my very core.

And while I was unsure of my feelings for Clark, my feelings for Max were just as strong as they had ever been. We had basically grown up together and even when I was married to Peter, I still had a small part of my heart that would always be Max's. I always thought that part would be dedicated to friendship, but here we were dating again.

"Now, in the past few years the medallion has been found by Gerald Pinkerton," Max said. Before he could continue on, there were several shouts and jeers from the crowd.

"He's a cheater," Lennie Mickelson yelled from the front of the crowd. Lennie was actually an out of towner who was in town just for the festival and the medallion hunt. I had talked to him that morning, he had been passionate about finding the medallion.

"Gerald is a fraud," Charlie said at the same time. Charlie, his siblings, and his father Rich owned the new bar in town called the Loony Bin. When I say new, I mean the newest bar that opened several months ago but will be the "new" bar until another one opens sometime. I didn't know much about

Charlie, but I did know that he had been talking a big game around town about finding that medallion and winning the prize.

"Now hold on there," Max said. "Let's not be throwing out accusations. Each year is a new competition and each year is a new chance for everyone to try and win the medallion hunt."

Charlie made his way through the crowd until he was standing next to Lennie. They looked at each other and nodded, each seeming to recognize that while they were in solidarity about Gerald being a cheater, they were still rivals when it came to finding the medallion.

"There is no possible way that he has found the medallion every single year without cheating," Lennie said. "I participate in medallion hunts all over the state and have never seen one where the same person wins every single time."

At this point, I started to look around to try to find Gerald. I finally spotted him towards the back of the crowd with a giant smirk on his face. He didn't seem to care about the accusations. Either he was actually a cheater or he was just very secure in his medallion hunting abilities.

"Come on guys," Max said. His pleading wasn't a sad sort of plea, but instead was more of a stern warning for them to stop. He had on his police officer voice. "If you are finished, I'd love to get on with sharing the first clue."

Charlie and Lennie glanced at each other with a look that said they both still thought Gerald was cheating, but that they didn't want to do much about it.

"Before I give you the first clue, let me remind you how it works," Max said. "Every morning this week until the medallion is found, a clue will be printed in the Shady Lake Tribune. The medallion is within the city limits of Shady Lake."

The crowd was growing restless. Looking around, you could tell who was going to really hunt for the medallion by who was hanging on Max's every word. Curiously, Gerald seemed to be calm, cool, and collected when compared to the other jittery participants.

"Here is the first clue: You are close to the mark if you are in one of Shady Lake's park."

I did a little eye roll at the not quite rhyme. Max never had been a very good writer. I know that the clues start very general and become more specific as the week goes on, but that was a bit too general. Shady Lake was full of parks. In Minnesota, you could find parks everywhere. I felt like the only thing this clue really told us was that it wasn't downtown.

"One more reminder," Max said. "Please be safe as you search. This is a fun competition, so don't take it too seriously."

Winter Festival Murder

A murmur ran through the crowd as the townspeople talked about the clue and where they were going to search. I turned and looked at Clark, who smiled down at me.

"Are you going to search?" I asked him.

"I might go out a few times," Clark said. "But I like to wait to really look until a few more clues come out otherwise I don't really know where to start looking. As a local, I may enlist your help."

Clark winked at me and I blushed a little bit. He made me so anxious, but in a good way.

On stage, Max had handed the microphone back to Ronald who was standing at the front of the stage, waiting for the crowd to settle down a bit. He had a big grin on his face, like usual.

"Shady Lakers, I would like to say one more thing," Ronald said. "I'd like to invite the winner of the medallion hunt for the last five years to come to the stage and share a few tips for searching for the medallion."

The crowd went silent as Gerald made his way to the stage. If looks could kill, Gerald would have millions of imaginary daggers flying at him right now. He seemed totally oblivious to it and made his way up the stairs and to the microphone.

"Hello there," Gerald said. "I can give you all one tip while you search which is to just keep at it. Don't give up. All of my other tips, I'm not going to tell you because I am also looking for the medallion this year and I don't want to give all of my secrets because I would love to win again. Scratch that. I am going to win again."

When Gerald spoke, he had a way of making you hate him. If he was a bit more sincere as he spoke I would assume that he was someone who enjoyed the medallion hunt, but instead he had this sort of sneer on his face that was easy to hate.

"So to all of you out there, you can hunt as much and as hard as you'd like, but I will once again be the winner."

That seemed to be just too much for the crowd. Looking around, most people were throwing a glare in Gerald's direction. Charlie and Lennie especially looked furious. Gerald smirked at all of the hate, seeming to be feeding off of it. Even Clark was giving him a nasty look.

"Good luck everyone," Gerald said with an evil smirk. That seemed to push the crowd over the edge.

"I swear if you find the medallion you'll be sorry," Lennie yelled.

"You watch your back Gerald Pinkerton," Charlie yelled.

Max walked up and snatched the microphone away from Gerald, pushing him back towards the stairs to get off of the stage.

"Now listen all of you, this is a fun

competition," Max said. "Don't you dare ruin this for everyone."

Charlie looked a bit ashamed. He stared at his feet, which he was shuffling a little bit. I spotted his father, Rich, shooting him a look from a different part of the crowd. Charlie must have noticed it too because his demeanor changed instantly.

Lennie on the other hand just gave a sort of shrug. He wasn't from Shady Lake, so he didn't care that much. He was simply here for the competition and Gerald was the one thing that seemed to be standing in his way.

Ronald took the microphone once more with a big smile on his face. He wasn't going to let anything get him down.

"I agree with Max," Ronald said. "Remember to keep things light and fun. Happy Below Zero Festival everyone!"

The crowd started to disperse, but I stood for a moment waiting to see if anything else happened. Gerald walked away and I wondered if he was going to start looking for the medallion right this minute. Charlie started to walk after him, but Lennie put a hand on his shoulder and stopped him. Together, they walked to the Loony Bin where I assumed they were going to share a drink and their hatred for Gerald.

Clark took my hand and squeezed it. When I

looked at him, he smiled. Cue the gooey feeling inside of me again.

"I think we need to find a cup of hot chocolate after all of that," Clark said. "We can discuss where we'd like to hunt for the medallion while we warm up a little."

As I let Clark lead me to the hot chocolate stand, I glanced once more towards the Loony Bin where Lennie and Charlie's retreating backs were just walking through the door. Imagine being so upset about a medallion hunt that you needed a drink to cool down.

Winter Festival Murder

•Chapter Three•

After the kickoff festival, each day was busy with activities. Monday night had a ceremony to crown the Below Zero Royalty. Instead of just having high school students compete, people of all ages competed for different titles. Teenagers competed to be Prince and Princess Icicle. Young adults competed to be King and Queen Blizzard and retired persons competed to be Duke and Duchess Avalanche. The entire idea would have been laughable if everyone was not so darn sincere about it.

What was a little different about this sort of ceremony was that it wasn't really a competition. It had nothing to do with skill or popularity, but instead the winners were chosen at random after a few fun rounds. It was enjoyable to know that it really was anyone's game and that no one would know who was going to win until the end.

My sister Tilly had decided to compete this year. She was a busy mother of three, but had decided that she needed something to focus her attention on outside of her house. When I asked her why in the world she had chosen this, she had shrugged and admitted that she just liked the idea that she wasn't actually going to be judged.

The entire ceremony was held in the high

school auditorium. About fifteen years ago, Shady Lake had built another high school to replace the crumbling old one. The auditorium in the "new high school" was big and beautiful. The acoustics were wonderful and there wasn't a bad seat in the house, not even up in the balcony. The seats were red velvet and actually pretty comfortable. They gave the sense that you could sit in one of the seats for the entirety of a long high school play without your bottom falling asleep.

The ceremony was so popular that the AV club set up a live feed so that people that came after the auditorium was full could sit in the cafeteria and still see everything. I had managed to snag a seat in the auditorium, but once I got there it was so full that only single seats remained, so I was not able to sit with Mandy or any of my family.

Across the auditorium, I spotted Rich and Sue sitting with Rich's children. I gave a wave and got an enthusiastic wave back. Just before I turned away, I saw Charlie come running down the side aisle towards the seat they had saved for him. He was pulling off a purple hat and a purple and yellow set of mittens when he saw his family waving. Charlie turned and gave me a wave also.

I ended up sitting next to Donna Grand, who worked in advertising at the local radio station. Every once in a while you'd hear her voice in an ad on the

Winter Festival Murder

AM station. Donna was a pretty, bubbly brunette who was curvy in all of the right ways. She was popular and funny, just the kind of person you wanted to sit next to during something as ridiculous at this ceremony.

While I was gone in college and living it up in the big city, Donna had become a single mother. She now had a three year old son, Bobby. While I didn't participate in the gossip around town, I did listen to it and I knew that no one really knew who Bobby's father was. I didn't think it really mattered because Donna was a great mother who showered her young son with love and affection.

Donna had told me that she had managed to get a babysitter for Bobby that night so she could come watch the ceremony. As someone who worked in media, she liked to know all everything that was going on in Shady Lake. Our talk soon turned to the medallion hunt.

"Are you going to search for it?" Donna asked. Her hazel eyes sparkled and her light brown hair sprung every which way, framing her ever youthful face.

"I'm not sure, but Clark did mention he might like my help to look," I said. "At least today's clue was a bit more helpful."

This morning, the clue in the paper had a bit more substance. It read:

Winter Festival Murder

<u>If the medallion is what you want to see,
Look in a park with a tree.</u>

It didn't seem helpful at first glance, but after I had read it a few times, I realized it wasn't saying that the park would have trees in it. Obviously all of the parks would have trees within them. The clue was saying that the park was named after a tree. That narrowed down the options quite a bit. Off the top of my head, I could think of at least five parks that were named after trees. There was Oak Park, Maple Park, Evergreen Park, Elm Park, and Birch Park. There were probably more, but considering there were about thirty parks in Shady Lake and less than half were named for trees, it did actually help.

"I've been going out to search on my breaks from work," Donna said with a smile. "I even took Bobby with me when I picked him up from school today."

"You are really dedicated," I said. "You must really enjoy the hunt."

"I'm not sure I'd say I enjoy it," Donna said. Her smile fell a little bit. "But that prize money would be really helpful. I don't want to complain about my salary because I love my job and the radio station pays me pretty well. But having a child is expensive and that prize money would be a big help for our bills."

"That is understandable," I said, patting

Donna's hand. "A little extra to help pay the bills is always welcome."

A few tears sprung to Donna's eyes and I pretended I didn't see them. I glanced at the stage, giving Donna time to wipe the tears away. As someone who has cried in public many times after Peter died, I know how embarrassing it is.

"Just so you know, I think you are doing an amazing job as a mother," I said quietly when I turned back to her. She squeezed my hand and gave me a shy smile as the lights in the auditorium went down to start the ceremony.

Ronald, of course, was the MC for the ceremony. He wobbled his way on stage with a microphone in his hand and a large smile on his face.

"Hello Shady Lake," he said. "Welcome to the Royalty Ceremony. Before we begin, I'd like to remind you that we are all here for fun. Please encourage everyone and keep this a fun atmosphere until we blind draw the winner."

He paused for some dramatic effect and some polite applause from the audience.

"Now, without much further ado, here are the contestants for this year's contest."

All of the contestants for the ceremony came out in a line and stood in one line across the middle of the stage. On their faces played a range of emotions, from excitement to nervous to complete terror. Tilly

Winter Festival Murder

looked mostly excited, but her eyes were darting around the auditorium. When I thought she was looking my way, I waved my hand frantically until she noticed and gave a little wave back. She was wearing a sparkly top, a knee length skirt, and her tap shoes. Tilly had danced as a child and still tried to join the adult tap dancing group occasionally. That skill would certainly come in handy tonight.

The ceremony had three parts. The first part was a trivia portion with trivia about Minnesota and Shady Lake. The contestants came up two at a time and went against each other to see who would win the best out of three. They kept narrowing down until there was a trivia winner in each age level.

Tilly did not do well in the trivia portion. She didn't seem nervous at all, which I admired. But she did slap her forehead when she couldn't remember the proper first name of the man who had established Shady Lake. I didn't really blame her. General Albert Custer was not notable for much else, partially because he wasn't a particularly nice man from what I remembered learning.

The next portion of the contest was the talent portion. Each contestant was tasked with coming up with a talent they could do in less than five minutes that had something to do with winter or cold. Tilly's tap dance was set to a jazzy Christmas carol and I thought she brought down the house. When she was done, I leapt to my feet to applaud and I'm pretty sure I wasn't the only one.

After each talent showcase, Ronald would come out with the microphone and lead the applause so each contestant got about the same amount. The talents ranged from Tilly's tap dance to a recitation of a winter poem to a comedy set about winter.

It was nice to sit next to Donna because after each contestant, she would lean over and we'd exchange a few words about how we thought each one did. At the beginning, Donna seemed tense, especially when we had discussed the prize money and her bills. But now she had relaxed and seemed to be enjoying herself. I was glad because as a single mother, I know she deserved a night out to have fun.

"That was our last talent for the night," Ronald said once Tim was done with his comedy set. "Let's bring everyone out and applaud them one more time."

All of the contestants came out for one more round of applause before the ceremony moved to the final stage: the random selection. Each age group was brought on stage and Ronald brought out a big fish bowl and a bunch of little bowls filled with pieces of folded paper.

One at a time, Ronald would dump a bowl in to choose one. He started with the high school Prince and then Princess. Then he moved on to the young adult King and Queen. I tried not to get too carried away when Tilly's name was called as this year's Queen Blizzard. Once the older adults had been crowned Duke and Duchess, the ceremony ended with one more round of applause for all of the contestants.

"That was so much fun," I said, turning to Donna. She was frowning at her phone, but quickly put it away when I spoke to her.

"What was that?" she said before realizing what I had said to her. "Oh yeah, this is one of my favorite parts of the festival every year. It is great to just watch everyone having fun without it being about popularity or who is better."

"It was nice to sit next to you Donna," I said as I threw my scarf around my neck and slipped my jacket on. "Good luck on your medallion hunt."

"Thank you Tessa," Donna said. "I can use all of the luck I can get because that prize money sure would help. I'll probably see you around more during this week. Have a good rest of your night."

I waved as I walked down the auditorium aisle. When I turned to look at her one more time, she had her phone out and was frowning at it once again. I hoped nothing was wrong with Bobby, but I figured if it was Bobby, she would be charging out of here instead of staring at her phone. I wasn't sure what was wrong, but I hoped everything was alright as I left to find and congratulate Tilly.

•Chapter Four•

The next morning, another clue came out in the newspaper. This one read:

<u>For the medallion to be seen,</u>
<u>Make sure you look somewhere green.</u>

Once again, this clue could be read several different ways, but one thing was for sure. All of the grass and plants were covered in snow. So this clue would help because most of the lampposts, garbage cans, and benches in the park were painted green. So it narrowed down the search a bit again.

That afternoon and evening were filled with outdoor hockey games. Hockey was a big deal in Shady Lake just as it was in most Minnesota towns. People followed the high school team almost like they were a professional team and it was adorable to see the younger kids be in total awe of these teenage hockey players. My teenage brother Tank plays defense for the high school team and while he just plays it off like it isn't a big deal, I know he loves all of the little fans that ask for his autograph after each game.

Most games were played in the ice arena on the edge of town. But during the Below Zero Festival, the team would play a special outdoor game on Shady Lake itself. Instead of a game that counted towards their actual record, this game was just for fun. They had arranged to play with the neighboring town, Waterville.

On the day of the game, I sat at the Donut Hut with Mandy and watched out the front window as they set everything up. A nice perk of being friends with the donut baker was a private donut snack after the donut shop was closed.

A couple of guys from the park and recreation department had been tasked with making the perfect ice rink out on the lake. They had taken some of the rink boards and set up the rink and then used colors to make all of the lines before moving the goals out onto the ice.

It was a bit nerve-wracking to watch them slowly drive the bleachers down the street. I hadn't put much thought into where everyone would sit for the game and the thought of putting bleachers on the ice terrified me. I was a lifelong Minnesotan and watching people drive their giant pickup trucks on the ice still made me cringe a little bit. Smaller cars weren't so bad, but the giant trucks were just so heavy. It did put my mind at ease when they set the bleachers up on the shore in the lakeside park.

"Okay, real talk," Mandy said as she set a cup of coffee in front of me. "Who do you think will win the hockey game tonight? Obviously I'm cheering for Shady Lake, but Waterville has been having a really strong year this year."

I gave Mandy a sharp look. Leave it to her to try to be nice to our rivals. Obviously I prefer a good, clean, Minnesota nice rivalry, but there was no way I'd admit that Waterville was good at hockey.

"If you are going to say nice things about Waterville, I will not be saving you a seat tonight," I said.

I grew up in a hockey family. All five of us had played hockey when we were little, but only Teddy, Trina, and Tank had continued playing through high school. We still got together to watch hockey, both college and professional games. It didn't really matter who was playing sometimes as long as it was a good game.

"Is Trevor off tonight?" I asked. "Is he coming with you to the game?"

"He told me he was going to come, but he's been pretty busy looking for the medallion," Mandy said.

Leave it to Trevor to be looking for an easy way to make money. I rolled my eyes a bit, trying to ignore Mandy's warning look. Trevor was her long time boyfriend. They been together since just after we graduated high school and really, the only thing I found redeeming about him was that he managed to keep a full-time job as an emergency dispatcher. Other than that, he seemed to be mostly a lazy, loaf-about. I tried to keep my mouth shut about it because Mandy really did love him and if she was happy, so was I. But it didn't mean I had to really like him.

I finished my coffee and my afternoon donut and bid Mandy goodbye. I knew when I got home, it would be time for everyone to get themselves decked out and bundled up for the game. Obviously we had to make sure we could stay warm while also declaring our undying support for the Shady Lake hockey team.

A few hours later, I was sitting on a cold metal bleacher saving a seat for Mandy and Trevor. I was bundled in more layers than I could count but over my jacket, I had a big, knit bright red and blue scarf. Shady Lake High School's colors were cherry and blue, which was a fancy way to say red and blue. I also had a blue hat with a big, red pom-pom that said Shady Lake across the front of it.

After a few minutes of shivering to myself in the bleachers, I spotted Mandy and Trevor coming my way. I waved until they saw me and figured out that it must be Tessa under all of my layers. Trevor was wearing a big, gray jacket and a gray stocking cap, but his outfit was lightened up by the purple and yellow mittens he was wearing. His love of football overrode his love of monotonous outerwear, apparently. Mandy was wearing a stylish and warm light blue puffer jacket and she was inexplicably carrying two large, red, outdoor chair cushions.

"Thank you so much for saving us some spots," Mandy said. "We got here as soon as we could. I had to wait for someone to come back from his medallion hunt for us to bundle up and join you out here."

"You're welcome," I said, ignoring the jab I could have given Trevor. "But what is the cushion for?"

Mandy looked down at the chair cushion as if she had forgotten she was carrying it. I'm sure she was wearing at least two pairs of mittens, so I didn't blame her for not being able to feel anything through them.

"Oh, this is to save us from a cold bottom," Mandy said. "Unless you really enjoy the cold metal bleacher in which case it'll be more cushion for me."

"That's a great idea," I said, standing up from my spot.

Mandy put the cushion down and I sat on top of it. The other chair cushion was for my parents to sit on. Mandy had been right. It was much more pleasant than the metal bleacher because besides the warmth it provided, it was also quite a bit softer than the bench.

The secret to keeping warm at a hockey game, especially an outdoor one, is to sit really, really close together. This time I was sitting squashed between my mother and Mandy. Together, we warmed each other. We still had some time before the game actually started, so while we watched the teams warm up and practice, I decided to try and strike up a conversation with Trevor.

"How is the medallion hunt going?" I asked him. Even though Mandy was between us, we were squished so close together that he was almost right next to me.

"Oh, it is going well," Trevor said. "Obviously I haven't found it, but I have some good ideas about where it might be. I just wish I had a little bit more time to search for it."

"Yeah, that must be hard when you have a full time job getting in the way," I said.

"It would be nice to not have a 9 to 5 job," he said. "Maybe you could tell me about that."

Touché. I had to admit that his jab towards me actually made me like him a little more. My family sometimes spoke to each other with sarcasm and teasing, so I had a soft spot for someone who could throw a joke back my way.

"But I have a system for how I've been searching for the medallion and I think I'm getting really close," Trevor said.

"He's certainly been busy," Mandy said. "He's hardly been home lately."

Trevor got a sheepish look on his face, which he quickly covered by looking away. I scowled before I could stop myself, but thankfully I was wearing a scarf over my face so no one saw. Mandy still gave me a little glare as she knew what I had done without even having to see it. She knew me too well. Before either of us could do anything else about it, the sound of someone tapping on a microphone interrupted us.

"Hello everyone, welcome to the Below Zero hockey game," Ronald said. He was standing at center ice with his signature smile on his face. I couldn't tell where Melinda was, but I was sure she was scowling somewhere in the crowd beneath a hat and scarf.

"We are so happy to have you all here today," Ronald continued. "Thank you for coming for this friendly game, Waterville. Now, if you'd all please stand for the National Anthem."

Everyone stood up and removed their hats. George Anderson shuffled his way onto the ice and took the microphone from Ronald. George was well past retirement age and he had been singing the national anthem at hockey games for decades. I actually wondered if he'd been doing it since he was a student at Shady Lake High School and I made a mental note to ask Ronald about that just out of sheer curiosity.

We all turned to face the flag that one of the cheerleaders was holding up behind one of the hockey nets. George's anthem was beautiful and long, but not too long. He had been doing it so long that he knew exactly how to do the anthem justice.

Winter Festival Murder

"Let's play hockey," George exclaimed at the end. We all applauded him and settled ourselves down to watch the game.

The only bad part about not being at the arena was that I couldn't get my favorite food to eat while watching hockey: nachos. Those salty tortilla chips with the warm cheese they pump out of the machine. It was disgusting and also the most delicious thing to eat.

The first period was pretty touch and go. Waterville scored first, which is always a true test to see how determined our team is. The Shady Lake players were undaunted by it and came back to score two quickly in a row. We ended the first period being up 3-2.

The second period didn't have any goals, but was full of excitement. Tank and a Waterville defense player started gunning for each other and both ended up in the penalty box having almost started a brawl. My dad had a scowl on his face because he hated when Tank's temper got the best of him. I assumed he may also be scowling because he could no longer feel his feet.

After the second period, I had to get up to stretch my legs while they smoothed the ice out. I spotted Lennie next to the stand where they were selling coffee, so I went to get a cup and see how he was doing. He was wearing a black, leather coat with

Winter Festival Murder

a purple and yellow scarf on top. He must also be a football fan. He was also scowling down at a piece of paper in his hands.

"Hello Lennie," I said. "I'm a little surprised to see you at the hockey game. You've been so busy searching for the medallion lately that I didn't think you'd be here."

"How do you know I'm not searching while I'm here," he said dryly, his dark eyes boring into me.

Lennie could be a bit unnerving. He wasn't from Shady Lake, but he was here so often that we knew him well. He worked as a seed salesman and he was always around chatting up farmers and seed stores. Lennie was known for being a very serious man and right now he seemed very serious about whatever he was reading in the letter. I caught a glimpse of the envelope. It was from Shady Lake Bank and Trust.

"You've got a point," I said. I tried to think of something else to say but couldn't think of anything, so I decided to just move on. "Enjoy the rest of the game, Lennie, and I'll see you back at the B&B."

"Yup," Lennie said before he wandered off towards a patch of trees.

I watched his back as he walked away and I ordered myself a coffee. I actually ordered one for Mandy too because even though she didn't usually drink coffee in the afternoon, I knew she would want one today. Trevor could fend for himself.

The third period kept us sitting on the edge of our seats. Waterville scored to tie it up 3-3. We scored again followed by Waterville to make it 4-4. They went back and forth down on the ice, shooting on the goal without much success. They were running out of time.

With the clock running down, our center took the puck down the ice and everyone else followed. After a shot on goal, the puck bounced back to where Tank was patrolling the ice. He grabbed it up, noticed that there were only seconds left on the clock, and wound up to hit the puck as hard as he could towards the goal. The goalie leapt to try to deflect it with his arm, but missed.

The puck hit the back of the net and fell onto the ice inside the goal. I jumped out of my seat, yelling and hooting at the top of my lungs. Thankfully, I had already finished my cup of coffee a while ago or it would have been all over everyone around me.

The team were all celebrating, having jumped into a big dog pile on top of Tank. What an amazing end to the game. It was a great game for both teams, but I was so proud of Tank. I felt like nothing could bring down our family during this festival.

•Chapter Five•

Wednesday dawned with both a new clue and a new activity for the day. The clue in the paper read:
<u>Even though Christmas is done,</u>
<u>We can still have holiday fun.</u>
The other clues had been making sense to me, but this one was very confusing. After a few minutes of thinking about it, I shoved the clue to the back of my mind because I wasn't looking for the medallion anyways. I needed to focus on the festival activity that I was helping to set up today.

We decided to have something fun for the kids, so we were setting up a sledding event at one of the local parks. We were going to have hot chocolate available and a bonfire. It seemed like it would be a really fun time for both kids and adults. It had even snowed a few inches last night, which meant we would need to pack down the snow on the sled hill a bit, but the fresh snow would provide a soft place to fall.

I'm not usually a morning person, but something about the excitement of the week long festival had me up and ready to go in time to help serve breakfast to the guests. Most of the guests were grandparents who were back to visit grandchildren during the festival. The odd man out was Lennie, who scowled into his coffee and only picked at his breakfast. Usually his appetite was voracious, but I assumed the medallion hunt must be frustrating him into not eating.

As I cleaned up the dining room after the guests had left, I saw Max pull up in his car. He had a trailer attached that must have been carrying all of the supplies we would need for our sledding. My mom saw him too and gave me a nod, holding out her hand for my apron. I tossed it into her hand and ran over to the door where I had piled up my outdoor gear. I poked my head out the door and gave Max a wave so he knew I saw him.

I jumped into my snow pants and layered up with my jacket, scarf, mittens and hats. Thankfully today wasn't as cold as it was during the hockey game. Of course, not as cold simply means that it is above zero, but still below freezing.

Max's car was nice and warm. He smiled a big, handsome smile at me and gave me a kiss on the cheek before pulling the car out of the driveway and heading to the park. There was a large sledding hill at Evergreen Park where we would be sledding today.

"We are not going to get too cold today," Max said. "Check the bag by your feet."

I looked in the plastic bag that was sitting on the floor of the car. It was chock full of those instant hand and foot warmers you can buy at the gas station. I had to laugh. Leave it to Max to buy an entire bag full of them instead of just the few we would need.

We pulled into the parking lot at the top of the hill in the park and I got out to take a look at our area. There was a large hill, but it wasn't too steep. Other hills in town were just as big but were so steep that they still scared me as an adult to think about sledding down. But this one was a gentle slope that even younger children could enjoy. There was also a large, flat area between the slope of the hill and the parking lot where we could set up the hot chocolate and a bonfire to warm us up.

Max was already taking out the supplies from the trailer attached to his car. A big folding table was set up and I put some of the hot chocolate supplies on top. We didn't have the hot water yet, but we would go get it when it got closer to sledding time.

There was also a fire pit that Max immediately set up and got a fire going inside. There was no reason to wait on the fire. It would help us keep warm while we got everything ready. In fact, I got a few chairs out of the back of the trailer and after setting them up, I plopped myself down in one to warm myself.

"Taking a break already?" Max teased. He sat in the chair next to me and took my hand in his. For a few moments, we just stared at the fire. I had a flashback to some of the bonfires we went to together when we were in high school. In a small town like Shady Lake there isn't much for teenagers to do, especially activities that don't cost money. A bonfire was about the only thing that was consistently fun.

"What else do we have to do?" I asked.

"We can't get the hot water until it is much closer to the sledding time, but we can get the sleds out," Max said. "We should maybe sled down a few times also to make sure there are some paths for the kids and see if there are any areas we should maybe fence off."

One of the best parts of this activity was that while children were welcome to bring their own sleds along, we provided a large selection of sleds for children who may not be able to afford their own sleds. In the trailer we had long plastic toboggans, small plastic circle saucers, and even a few of the sleds that have little seats inside for smaller children.

In the very back of the trailer was some snow fencing that we could use to make a safe sledding course if we needed to. Looking down the hill, I was concerned about one group of evergreen trees in particular. There were three of them set behind a green park bench. I pointed them out to Max, who suddenly started to seem shifty.

"Oh yeah, that might be a problem," Max said. "I can be the one to put up a fence around that. I don't really need your help."

My mind flashed back to the medallion clue from that morning. It had mentioned Christmas and here we were at Evergreen Park. This is probably where Max had hidden the medallion, specifically it was probably down by that park bench at the bottom of the hill.

"That's where the medallion is, isn't it?" I asked.

Max looked around like someone might pop up and rush to the bench to get it. He started to grumble a little bit and kept gesturing with his hands without actually say anything. I would take this reaction as a yes, even if he wouldn't actually say it.

"Don't worry," I said. "I won't go get it. I think it would be cheating if I did that."

Max visibly relaxed when I said that, but he still looked a bit nervous. I don't think he had really thought through the fact that the medallion was here where we were also hosting a different activity. If he had, he may have moved one or the other to a different location.

"I think it will also help that there is a slight drift down there in front of the bench," I said, pointing down the hill. "See? If people can't really get to the bench, they may not find the medallion if you hid it well enough."

Max just shrugged at me. I got the sense that

even though I had figured it out, he didn't want to actually say that the medallion was down there. I decided not to push it.

"Let's get the rest of the chairs set up and then we can start testing the hill," Max said before he turned and walked back to the trailer where the chairs were leaning against the sides.

I rolled my eyes at his back and followed him to get the chairs set up. As soon as I did that, I could get to the fun part of sledding.

•Chapter Six•

Finally, it was time to test out the sled hill. I was getting my toboggan all set up to take the first run. We didn't want kids to get stuck in the new fluffy snow, so we were going to go down a few times to pack it down to make for some good sledding.

We had finished setting up most of the chairs around the bonfire and a few around the table with the hot chocolate. Besides going to get some hot water shortly before the event started, we were ready. So now we could take our turn at some good old fashioned sledding since we knew we would be mostly running security and safety during the actual sledding event.

I picked out a big, purple, plastic toboggan. Max told me I could take the first run and then he would come down behind me on a plastic saucer. He knew I was so excited that I could barely stand it. But could you blame me? Fresh snow and a fun hill with no one else to dodge around. It was a sledding dream.

I sat down and tried to angle the toboggan away from the bank of trees and the park bench that we were still considering putting a fence up in front of. We still had plenty of time to put it up if we decided it was necessary.

"1, 2, 3," I called as I used my hands to slide

back and forth to give myself some momentum.

I pushed myself off with my hands and grabbed onto the rope handle that was attached to the sled. I'm not sure why I held on to it other than I felt like I was supposed to. I don't think it would do much to help me steer if I needed to. It only provided a false sense of security.

Halfway down the hill, I hit a seemingly invisible little bump that sent me flying. I couldn't help but scream as it launched me into the air. I held on tight so that I wouldn't tip over and I landed with a bump that was hard enough to hurt my tailbone a bit. It didn't help that I couldn't see a thing. The crash back into the soft snow had sent snow up in a flurry. At least I was still upright.

I could hear Max yelling at me from the top of the hill, but I couldn't really hear what he was saying and I certainly couldn't see him. Then the snow cleared from my sight and I could see the problem. The unexpected air launch had changed the direction I was sledding in. Instead of clear down the middle, I was now headed straight for the bench and the pine trees we had been worried about.

The big snow drift we had spotted was still right in front of the bench, so I was hoping that would stop me instead of the bench. A big pile of soft snow would make for a much better crash than a hard park bench. To help myself slow down, I dropped the rope and stuck my hands out to the sides. As my mitten clad hands dragged in the snow, I started to slow down ever so slightly as I came up to the snow drift.

CRASH

Instead of the soft crash I had been expecting from the snowbank I ran into, I hit it head on and it was hard. I cartwheeled off of my toboggan, tumbling head over heels until I finally landed flat on my back. There was snow everywhere and my face was covered by it. Thankfully I had been thrown next to the park bench and not right up on top of it.

I lay still for a moment before brushing off my face, fully aware that as a thirty year old woman, that crash I would have jumped up from as a child was enough to break an arm. But nothing seemed to be hurt worse than my pride, so I sat up as I heard Max yelling.

"I'm coming Tessa, don't get up," Max yelled. His voice was deep and serious. He was not joking around after that crash.

I looked up the hill and saw that Max was flying down the hill on his red, plastic saucer, his knees bent up almost to his chin. He looked ridiculous and I couldn't help but laugh at him. He had on his serious business, Mr. Officer face so I sat still and tried to swallow back the rest of my laughter so I didn't offend him. I'd heard of bicycle cops and horseback cops, but never a sled cop. That was probably because they were much tougher to take seriously.

"Are you okay Tessa?" Max said as he jumped up off of his sled and ran over. I was a little bit impressed by how spry he was since we were the same age and I definitely wouldn't be able to just spring up off of the ground like that.

"Yes, I'm fine," I said. I took his hands and let him help me up. "I thought that snowdrift would be soft and help me have a soft crash landing that might hurt less than the bench, but I guess not."

"Yeah, there isn't anything in front of the bench normally and I can tell you that there wasn't anything there when I was here earlier in the week. Maybe we should see what it is so we can put a fence up."

I brushed myself off and we walked back towards the drift. What could be so hard under there? We couldn't have a kid running into something like that on their sled. So far the Below Zero Festival had a track record of no injuries and I'd like to keep it that way.

The lump was still all covered with snow when we looked at it except for a small area where the sled had hit. The snow had fallen off there and exposed a little bit of color that looked like some kind of fabric. It almost looked like someone had lost a jacket, except it was much bigger than that and even a frozen jacket wouldn't be big enough or hard enough to toss me

Winter Festival Murder

from my sled.

I knelt down and started to brush some snow off of one end of the lump while Max brushed snow from the area I had hit. After a bit of brushing, something sickly white was starting to emerge from the snow. There was some hair and some lumps. I jumped back and shrieked a bit as I realized that what I was brushing snow off of was actually a human face.

"Tessa, are you okay?" Max said. I looked at where he was brushing off snow and saw what I recognized now as an arm with a hand on the end covered by a purple mitten. Without the context of the face I had just found, Max couldn't tell what it was.

I pointed towards what I had just uncovered. Max glanced over and took a quick step back. His face went pale and his mouth dropped open.

"What in the world?" he exclaimed.

The dead body of Gerald Pinkerton was staring up at us. As we brushed the snow gently off of him, the rest of Gerald appeared. He was curled up in a fetal position and he appeared to be clutching his stomach. There was some red colored snow underneath his torso. We also managed to brush off a gun. I would bet money that once they investigated him a bit more, they'd find a gunshot wound in his stomach.

Max stood up and grabbed his phone to call for

backup from the rest of the police force.

"I don't think we will need to put up that fence," I said. "Because I don't think we will be doing any sledding here today."

•Chapter Seven•

Shortly after we discovered Gerald, several police cars came screaming up with lights flashing. I thought it was a bit much since it wasn't like the killer was hiding somewhere nearby. It was way too cold for that and Gerald had obviously been dead for a while. As Max told all of the officers about what we had found, I took that time to call the radio station and put out an all points bulletin that the sledding was canceled due to an undisclosed emergency.

Unlike the previous murders I had unfortunately stumbled upon, the nice thing about this one was that I had come across the body with a police officer so instead of being under suspicion, I was just asked about all of the details I remember.

After Max and I had each given our stories, we told them together to try to make sure our stories were the same. Of course it was pretty hard to get the "Tessa sledding into the dead body" story wrong. We retold our story several times, when suddenly I remembered something.

"Max, you didn't actually confirm this, but was the Below Zero medallion hidden in this park?" I asked. "I assume that's why Gerald would be here. Do you think someone shot him for the medallion?"

Max's face drained of color. I got the distinct

idea that he had not even considered the medallion until I said something. But it made perfect sense to me. Gerald seemed to be pretty universally hated for always finding the medallion. He'd been found here, so he had probably found it and someone followed him to it. I'm not sure why someone would kill over a medallion, even if it was worth $500, but I wasn't the one who did it so of course I don't understand.

"Okay fine, I did hide the medallion here," Max said after a long pause. He looked pained to have to admit that. "It is just so hard because I spend a long time finding a good hiding place and making sure it isn't super obvious. I'll check the hiding spot, but if it is still there the medallion hunt will be ruined."

"I'm pretty sure the dead body next to the medallion's hiding place has already put a damper on the event," I said before I could stop myself. Max shot me a look that told me to shut my big mouth, but one of the other police officers, a young guy named Philip, hid a snicker from him.

Max sighed a big sigh. With how many parks Shady Lake has, I was pretty sure it wasn't actually that difficult to hide the medallion, but Max was acting like it was his life's work. I tried not to roll my eyes at the dramatics of it.

He walked over to the park bench and with a furtive look around, he bent down and looked underneath. Max brushed off a little spot right next to the leg of the park bench. After a moment, he quickly swept all of the snow out from underneath the bench.

"It isn't here," he called. "I thought maybe it was just hidden under the snow, but it is totally gone."

So whoever killed Gerald probably had the medallion, unless Gerald had the medallion on him right now. Of course, I wasn't going to go search his dead body, but I hoped I could get Max to at least tell me that much information later.

Max walked back over to me and grabbed my hand. He didn't usually like to show affection around his fellow police officers, but he wasn't on duty and the shock of finding Gerald must have allowed him to let his guard down a little.

We watched them load Gerald's body into a black body bag and carry it back up the hill. We each grabbed the sled we had come down the hill riding, although the joy of the sled ride seemed so far away now. When we got to the top of the hill, I was pleased to see that the other officers had loaded up the trailer with all of the tables, chairs, and sleds that we had brought with us.

"Come on Tessa, I'll give you a ride home," Max said.

He walked me to the passenger side door and opened it for me. I slid down into the seat and smiled while I waited for Max to shut the door and walk around the car. No matter what, Max always insisted on opening my car door for me. I typically didn't care for the "chivalry, macho" kind of attitude, but coming from Max it just seemed more natural.

"Let's take a drive first," he said. "I need a few moments to clear my head."

By now, it was late afternoon and it was starting to get late. As the sun was going down, outdoor light displays around town were starting to light up. It seemed to help cut through the dreary middle of a Minnesota winter.

I reached over and put my hand on Max's arm as he drove. When I looked at his face, it was set in a stony expression that I was having trouble reading. I'd known Max for so long that I could usually tell what he was thinking. But this mix of emotions was new.

"Was that the first time you've found a body?" I asked quietly. Obviously as a police officer, he had dealt with murders and dead bodies before. But I imagine stumbling across one in your personal life was a bit different from when he was on duty. Unfortunately stumbling across dead bodies was becoming something that was happening way too often for me.

"It was the first time I'd found a body like that," he said. His entire body seemed to stiffen up. "I was the one that found Anne after she passed."

Winter Festival Murder

   Anne was Max's first wife who had died of
cancer around the same time my husband had died.
Why had I asked him such a stupid question? Max
and I seemed to have an unspoken agreement to not
talk about each other's previous spouses. I would
occasionally share a funny anecdote about Peter and
Max would share a sweet story about Anne, but never
had I asked him about Anne.
   "I'm so sorry Max," I said. "I wasn't thinking
when I asked that question."
   "It's okay Tessa," he said. But the tone in his
voice had changed. "I don't like to think about it, but I
know that you didn't mean it in a bad way."
   We sat in silence for a while as we drove
around Shady Lake. I tried to think of something to
say to Max, but I didn't know what to say. I'd let my
mouth do the thinking and it got me in trouble again.
I tried to take Max's hand, but he pulled his hand out
from my grasp. My spirits instantly sunk and I hoped
I hadn't put a permanent kink in our relationship.
   As we wound around the lake, I watched more
and more lights pop on. I tried to focus on them and
how happy they looked instead of focusing on the
tension in the car. It started to snow just as we got to
my house, which made the B&B even more beautiful.
The holiday light display that we had set up for the
Christmas light contest was still up and it made me
smile as I saw it illuminated because I had worked

hard on it.

The Shady Lake Bed and Breakfast was an old Victorian house that had been given new life by my parents after most of us kids had moved out. It was a white house with green shutters that they repainted each summer. The porch had evergreen plants to decorate for the winter and each window that was facing the street had a fake candle lit up on the windowsill. I thought that with the snow falling, it looked like a scene from one of the puzzles we usually put together on Christmas.

Max pulled into the driveway and turned the engine off. For a moment, we sat in silence. I had a bad habit of sticking my foot in my mouth, but this time I had really done it. I had no idea how to make up for this one, but I thought an apology would be a good place to start.

"I'm sorry again Max," I said. I couldn't help but apologize again. In fact, I'd probably apologize ten more times because I felt so terribly. "I really didn't mean to hurt you."

"I know," Max said. He was looking everywhere except at me and his tone was flat. "I accept your apology, Tessa. I know you wouldn't hurt me again."

Max got out of the car and walked around to my side to open my car door up. Together, we ran through the cold wind up to the front door where he gave me a quick peck goodbye as I went inside. I pulled my snowy boots off and threw them on the entry rug before running to the front window in the living room to wave him goodbye.

I waved frantically and when Max looked up, he gave me one firm wave of his hand. I recognized that look on his face now. It wasn't because I had known him for so long but because I had seen that face on myself in the mirror. Grief is funny and it pops up when you least expect it. Today, I had caused it to pop up for Max. And now the look on his face said that he was trying to deal with it as much as possible instead of just stuffing it away.

That was why he had mentioned me not hurting him again. When I had left for college and eventually broken up with him because of the distance, he had been really hurt. Now, I had ripped the band aid off of that old wound also.

Poor Max. I would give him a little time before I reached out. I knew from personal experience that after a time like this, you need a little time to grieve by yourself before you let someone reach out and pull you up and out of the muck.

For now, I'd just have to deal with finding a dead body on my own.

Chapter Eight

I had only been home for a little while when I got a text from Mandy.

I've been waiting for you to text me and tell me about whatever mysterious emergency requiring almost the entire Shady Lake police force made you shut down the sledding event. I'm dying over here!

If you asked Mandy, she would say that she wasn't a gossip, but she was always willing to discuss facts. Personally, I didn't see much difference between the two but Mandy was very careful to never just pass on idle gossip she picked up. She would always try to verify with the source or at least a few other people that were in the know before she would share it with anyone else.

To me, that was still gossiping. But Mandy insisted that it wasn't. I sent her back a quick message.

Are you home? Maybe I'll pick up some pizza and we can have dinner together.

Mandy agreed and after I told my mother my plan, I steered my station wagon through the pitch black to Mike's Pizza. Normally, I would order ahead, but I knew that they always had a few plain old cheese and pepperoni pizzas waiting for people like me who wanted to grab it on the way somewhere.

I got back in the car with the hot pizza, glad

Winter Festival Murder

that Mandy's apartment over the Donut Hut was only a few blocks away because the pizza smelled delicious. Mike's was a town favorite and it had been for decades. The secret to their success was that they used slices of cheese instead of shredded cheese on top. Between that and the super catchy jingle they played on the local radio station, chain pizza stores could hardly compete.

Mandy shared her apartment with Trevor who I think should thank his lucky stars every single day for Mandy because while at least he has a job, he is not much of a housekeeper. Trevor moved in with Mandy straight from his mother's house shortly after high school and he had never quite learned how to care for himself. But between the fact that Mandy is just naturally tidy and that neither of them own much, their apartment is always spotless.

When Mandy's parents moved to Florida and left her in charge of the Donut Hut, Mandy decided to live in the apartment on top of the shop. Her parents had always rented it out for some extra income, but Mandy decided she liked the free place to live more than the extra income that would just go towards the mortgage anyways.

The apartment was small, but cozy and cute. From the door in the back of the Donut Hut, you walked up a set of stairs that Mandy had painted a lilac color. The walls were covered with anything

Mandy could find with donuts, whether it was artwork with donuts or a small carved donut. I thought it was a bit much, but Mandy pointed out that she spent so much of her life dealing with donuts that this way she could leave it all behind her when she got to her apartment door.

I walked up and straight into her apartment. The entryway was narrow, but it had enough room for a vintage, wooden coat rack that inexplicably stood up no matter how much outerwear was thrown on it. There was a skinny table with a bowl on top of it that held Mandy's car keys and a spare pack of gum. Above the table was a mirror that I used and appreciated in the winter when I had been wearing a hat and needed to make sure I looked halfway presentable. I smoothed down my crazy hair and carried the pizza into the next room.

"Hey Tessa," Mandy called. "I've already got plates and stuff out so just bring the pizza into the kitchen."

I walked through Mandy's minimalist living room to get to her kitchen. The kitchen was simple also. Mandy always said that if she needed anything else, she could run downstairs and cook so what was the sense in cluttering up her living space? Her kitchen had open shelving that held all of her dishes and her pots and pans hung on a rack above a very small butcher block island in the center of the galley kitchen.

I plopped the pizza down on top of the island and opened it up. The smell that wafted out made my mouth water and I gave myself an imaginary pat on the back for deciding to pick up a pizza on the way.

"Trevor should be home any minute, but we can start eating," Mandy said, popping her gum a few more times before spitting it out into the garbage. I tried not to roll my eyes at the thought of Trevor coming. There is no way I had been planning on waiting for him before I dug into this pizza.

Mandy put a slice of pizza on each of the plates she had out and handed one to me along with a fork. I had grown up eating everything with a fork because my mother hated to get her hands dirty and I hadn't realized how weird that was until I was older and it was fully ingrained in me and much too late to stop.

We moved out into the living room which was my favorite part of Mandy's apartment. The large windows looked out over one of the streets of Shady Lake's quaint downtown. All of the buildings had been at least partially restored and when it was winter, they were all outlined in strands of white Christmas lights. All of the lampposts had large, shimmery snowflakes on them with banners advertising the Below Zero Festival. Downtown felt historic and vivacious all in one glance.

The decade I had spent out of town had been

the start of a large local push to revitalize downtown. What used to be a bunch of old buildings with struggling businesses was now a beautiful area of local shopping that drew in people from all over Southern Minnesota. Shady Lake had started a program that gave out loans to small businesses to help them revitalize their old, crumbling buildings. They had also formed a small business mastermind group that helped some of the struggling businesses come up with a business plan and new ways to draw in customers.

If you looked out the windows to the left, there was a great view of Shady Lake. Right now, the snowy white of the frozen lake was broken up by dark blobs that I knew to be ice houses. In the summer, we would open the windows and we could hear the sounds of warm-weather fun from people out boating. It was like a more subdued version of the hip, inner-city apartment where I had lived with Peter.

I took in the beautiful, snowy view from my perch on Mandy's tufted, dark blue sofa. Mandy settled herself into a mustard yellow armchair that was arranged facing the windows. In front of us was a large, wooden cable spool that they used as a coffee table. The thing I loved about Mandy's decorating style is that she knew exactly how to use the cable spool to make the formal furniture more casual.

Winter Festival Murder

"How is Trevor's medallion hunt going?" I asked.

I knew he had been spending so much time out searching, but as soon as I said it, I got a sick feeling in the pit of my stomach. Someone had killed Gerald over the medallion. Maybe Trevor knew who did it. Or maybe he had even been the one to do it. The piece of pizza I had in my mouth seemed to turn to glue as I tried to chew it enough to swallow down.

"Well, he hasn't found it yet," Mandy said, oblivious to my internal torment. "But he has been out searching every night. In fact, he's been so dedicated that he was out last week scouting out possible hiding places before the medallion had even been hidden. I'm really proud of him for taking the initiative to do something like that. Usually he needs my encouragement to do things."

I rolled my eyes as Mandy shot a scowl at me. I realized that I was actually there to tell her about Gerald, so I launched into the story. Mandy kept biting her lip, which was a pretty big sign that she already knew the story somehow. She usually tried to act innocent so that people would give her more information, but I knew that when she chewed on her lip, the innocent thing was all an act. I still told her the whole story.

I finished with telling her about how I had inadvertently upset Max but before Mandy could respond, her phone dinged to say that there was a message. Mandy took our her phone and as her eyes darted around the screen, her mouth dropped open and she started to cry.

"What's wrong Mandy?" I asked, setting my pizza down on my plate.

Instead of answering, Mandy handed her phone to me. On the screen was a message from Trevor that simply read:

Emergency. Police are questioning me about Gerald's murder. I didn't do it. Help please.

•Chapter Nine•

I tried not to roll my eyes again, but how did Trevor expect us to help? Did he want us to bust down the courthouse doors armed with machine guns so we could grab him and skip town? I scoffed to myself, but I stopped when I glanced over at Mandy.

Mandy was sitting in the chair with tears silently running down her face. I handed her back her phone. I wasn't sure what to say to her. If Trevor was being questioned by the police, we couldn't just go get him. We would have to wait for him to be released. I reached over and patted her hand a couple of times, trying to assess what she needed in this moment in time.

"What am I going to do Tessa?" Mandy asked after a few moments of silence. "Trevor didn't do this. You need to help me."

Mandy looked at me and her face was a mask of despair. I was torn inside about what to say. I wanted to comfort her, but I really didn't know what to do to help.

"I'm not sure how to help you, Mandy," I said. "If he is being held by police, we can't just go get him."

Tears kept falling down Mandy's face as she

worked from crying to sobbing. I stood up and ran to the bathroom to grab a box of tissues for her. Mandy grabbed a few and wiped her face as she sobbed.

I moved to the end of the sofa and reached out to hold Mandy's hand again. Throughout our friendship, we had been through a lot of times like this. We had cried together over boys, family, speeding tickets, failed tests, and death. This was a bit different. I had always thought that if Mandy was crying over Trevor, it would be because he dumped her. Neither of us had seen this coming.

After a few moments, I leaned over and wrapped Mandy in a big bear hug. She pulled me to sit next to her in the armchair. We stared out the window at the falling snow as Mandy's tears slowed to a drip, her head sitting on my shoulder.

"Tessa, I need to ask you a big favor," Mandy said quietly, keeping her head snuggled up into the crook of my neck.

"Anything Mandy," I said. "You know that you are more like a sister than a friend. I would do anything to help you."

"I need you to find something that shows that Trevor didn't do it," Mandy said. "I know he didn't do it and I need you to help me prove that to the police."

I sucked my breath in through my teeth before I could stop myself, causing Mandy to start sobbing a bit more again. I knew I would have to investigate, which was turning into something I was doing way too often. I mean, I like true crime podcasts, but somehow I kept falling into real life true crime to figure out.

"I know you don't like him," Mandy said when I didn't answer her. "But I love him. I love Trevor and I can't imagine my life without him."

"Isn't love funny?" I said, voicing what should have been a silent musing. Mandy didn't seem to notice. "Of course I will help you. No matter what my thoughts are on Trevor, I will help because I love you."

"Thank you Tessa," Mandy said.

The smell of the pizza wafted towards me again and I realized that I hadn't even finished my first slice of pizza. I stood up from the armchair and grabbed our plates. I got us each another piece of pizza and I sat back down on the couch, handing one plate to Mandy. The next step we took needed to be making some sort of plan.

It was almost too late to do anything that night besides talk about investigating. January in Minnesota was dark almost all of the time, which meant time to investigate was limited. But we decided to go together the next day to check out the scene of the crime.

"Are you going to be alright Mandy?" I asked after our second slices of pizza were gone. It was getting later and I knew I should be getting back to the bed and breakfast, but I wasn't going to leave if Mandy was in distress.

Mandy sniffed a few times and wiped her face once more with a tissue. She took a few deep breaths to calm down and then nodded her head.

"I'll be alright Tessa," she said. "I need to get to bed anyways. It is almost my bed time and the donuts won't bake themselves tomorrow."

I stood up and cleaned up the plates and leftover pizza while Mandy sat and collected herself. When I came back from the kitchen, she stood up and walked me to the entryway. She grabbed a stick of gum from the bowl in the entryway. Only Mandy would chew a piece of gum right before she brushed her teeth, but whatever she needed to do to feel better.

As I put on my jacket, Mandy rifled through my purse and pulled out the large, metal flashlight I kept in there. Ever since Peter died, I found myself scared of the dark. To combat that, I kept flashlights everywhere. Once my jacket was on and zipped and my hat placed firmly on my head, Mandy handed me my purse and the flashlight.

I walked out of her door into the little donut hallway with the staircase, but I turned and wrapped her in one last hug. Mandy has always been smaller than I am and I tend to smother her with my love, but

Winter Festival Murder

she usually doesn't mind.

"I will come as early as I can tomorrow to see how you are doing," I said. I couldn't promise to come when she was awake because she woke up in the wee early hours of the morning to make donuts for the town. But I would come early to see how she was doing and help out if she needed.

Mandy nodded and waved goodbye. I stood in the little hallway until I heard her lock the door. I wanted to make sure she kept herself safe, even though Shady Lake typically didn't have much crime.

I pushed the little rubber button on the flashlight and took a deep breath before I walked down the stairs, slowly plunging myself into the winter darkness. At the bottom of the staircase, I tentatively opened the door and shone my flashlight around the alley. There was nothing there except my station wagon and some dumpsters.

I dashed to my car and unlocked it as fast as I could, which was never fast enough. I fumbled the keys a few time as I could feel my nerves start to make my hands shake and my stomach start to feel sick. Finally, the key went into the lock and I was able to turn it. I shone my flashlight into the backseat to make sure there wasn't someone back there, which was something I always did after hearing a story of a killer waiting in someone's backseat for them to get back in the car.

Winter Festival Murder

As I slid into my seat and shut the door, I quickly turned on the car and my headlights. Only then was I able to sit and grip the steering wheel, taking a few deep breaths to calm myself after the tension of the darkness that felt like it had been closing in.

Once I felt calm enough, I pulled my car out of the alley and onto the street. I glanced up at Mandy's apartment window and I was happy to see that the lights were out, which meant she was going to bed. She needed to rest and try to get her mind off of Trevor and his problems.

The lake was dark, with only moonlight to illuminate it. It was quite calming, especially because hardly anyone was out on this cold, cold Minnesota night. I was the only car on the road on the way home and I was happy with that. It meant I could drive as slow as I wanted while looking at the lights.

I spent the drive home thinking about the murder. This one might be tough because in one sense, anyone who had been looking for the medallion could be a suspect. But I don't think just any casual medallion searcher would kill over it.

Gerald must have found the medallion, but someone must have been following him and killed him for it. Now the only question was who would do that? And why was the medallion worth killing over?

•Chapter Ten•

The next morning, I stopped by the Donut Hut bright and early. As I walked in, I spotted Donna in the small corner booth. I normally would have just given her a little wave, but she looked quite upset, so I stopped by her booth because I could see that Mandy was busy behind the counter. Donna didn't even notice I was standing there at first.

"Donna, are you alright?" I said quietly. I knew from experience how embarrassing it was to be caught crying in public and I didn't want to draw a bunch of attention to her.

Donna looked up, a look of surprise on her face. She opened her mouth to speak, but instead, she whimpered a bit and a few more tears rolled down her face. I quickly sat down in the spot across from her so that I would partially cover her from anyone else.

"You don't have to tell me what is wrong, but just know that I am here if you need to talk," I said.

After nodding a few times, Donna took a drink of coffee and finally spoke.

"I know everyone wonders who Bobby's father is," Donna said. "And I'm not ready to share that, but I did get some bad news about him. I had been hoping he would pay more child support to help, but he isn't able to. Between that and the medallion hunt going wrong..."

Donna trailed off as the tears started to flow again. I reached across the table and gave her hand a firm squeeze. She grabbed a napkin and dried her tears while I tried hard to shield her from everyone else at the Donut Hut.

"Thank you Tessa," she said. "I really should be getting to work. I was just feeling sorry for myself this morning and thought I'd be able to sit in public, but it all really just hit me."

"You must be disappointed about the medallion hunt," I said. "I know you were really getting into it."

"Yes I am," Donna said. "Poor Gerald."

Donna's face fell as she thought about Gerald, which was surprising to me. While obviously any sort of murder is not condoned, Gerald wasn't exactly someone who seemed like he was going to be missed. I wondered if Donna had some other connection to Gerald, but I wasn't going to ask her that now.

We both stood up and said our goodbyes. Donna headed towards the door and I headed towards the counter. Mandy seemed to be mostly back to her cheerful self when I got to the register. She sent me off with a travel mug full of coffee, a donut with blue frosting and snowflake sprinkles, and a promise to text me when the shop closed for the day. I took out my phone and made sure the ringer was on. I had switched to a flip phone and I liked it, but the worst part was that I continually hit the "silence" button that was inexplicably on the outside of the phone. I'm not sure who designed this phone, but they did not do a great job of it.

When my phone dinged with a message later on that morning while I was cleaning the living room at the bed and breakfast, I was surprised to see that it was from Trevor, not Mandy. I only had Trevor's number in my phone in case Mandy ever had an emergency and I'm sure it was the same sort of reason that he had my number. We had never called or texted each other before. But today, he sent me a message.

Tessa, I need to meet with you. You need to help me. For Mandy. Meet me for some tacos for lunch.

I sat back for a moment and thought about it. If nothing else, I do need to do what I can to help Mandy. Plus I could really go for some tacos for lunch. I sent Trevor back a message telling him I would see in a bit.

An hour later, I walked into the Taco Queen and spotted Trevor sitting at the table in the window. I gave him a wave and went to order my lunch. I wasn't sure if he picked that table on purpose, but it was the exact same table that Max and Mandy and I had eaten lunch at every day in high school. Trevor went to high school with us, but at that point we hardly knew him. It was only after I left town for college that he and Mandy started dating.

I ordered my taco salad and brought my plastic number to the table. Trevor was leaned back in his chair, slumping over occasionally to sip his pop. I plopped down across the table from him and waited for him to talk.

Trevor had been a skateboarder in high school with long, shaggy hair and the baggy clothes to match. I honestly hadn't known anything about him back then, but I don't think he's changed much. His dark hair was still shaggy, but shorter as his job as an emergency dispatcher required him to look somewhat professional. Since he wasn't at work, he was wearing a baggy pair of jeans, a t-shirt, and a zip-up hoodie. If you didn't know he was thirty years old, you never would have guessed it. I wondered if anyone had ever accused him of skipping school after he had already graduated.

"I need your help Tessa," Trevor finally said. He spoke quietly and I had trouble hearing him over the din of the lunch crowd, so I leaned forward. "I can't tell Mandy what I was doing but I promise you that I didn't kill Gerald."

"What exactly were you doing?" I asked.

Trevor grabbed his pop and took a sip. I sat back and waited. I could almost see him weighing what to do back and forth in his mind.

"I will tell you," Trevor said. "But you have to promise not to tell Mandy."

A few thoughts raced through my head. Mandy and I told each other everything. I wasn't going to keep something bad from her. I know I thought of Trevor as an idiot, but what if he told me he was cheating on Mandy? Did he really expect me to keep something like that from her?

The waiter came over and delivered my taco salad and I used that as an excuse to take a little more time while I put my dressing over the top. As much as I love plain old tacos, the taco salad at Taco Queen was to die for. It came with both ranch dressing and salsa to top it with along with tortilla chips which I crumbled on top of it all.

Trevor ate another taco, seemingly nonplussed about the fact that I hadn't yet answered him. To get any further with him, I would have to agree to not tell Mandy. But I hated the fact that I may have to break that promise depending on what he told me.

"Okay, hit me with it," I finally said. I took another big bite of salad so that I couldn't mouth off depending on what he said.

"I know I've made kind of a big deal about searching for the medallion," Trevor said. "But I actually haven't searched for it because I've..."

Trevor trailed off and I mumbled a bit, which I

couldn't hear over the din of lunchtime noise around us.

"What?"

"I've been studying," he said.

"Studying for what?" I said, a bit too loudly. Trevor looked around furtively, as if he didn't want anyone to know he had been studying.

"Studying for the entrance exam at the community college," he said through his teeth, trying to keep it so that no one could hear him, as if going back to school was something to be ashamed of. I guess it seemed like that if your entire personality had been based on being a slacker.

"I think that's wonderful," I said. I wasn't sure what else to say. I was glad he wasn't cheating on Mandy, so that was something.

"Yeah, but I don't want to tell Mandy yet, just in case I fail," Trevor said. "I need to pass the exam and then when I do, I'm going to surprise her. She's been pushing me to go back to school because I've been talking about it for a while, but it's taken some time to actually do anything about it."

Trevor and I both went back to eating for a moment while I thought things through. Trevor munched through another taco while I took a bite of salad.

"Trevor, I have to say that I really admire you for going back to school," I said finally. "I think I've underestimated you and I apologize for that. So now I'm wondering what you'd like me to do."

This time, it was Trevor's turn to stall. As I spoke, Trevor's face broke into a genuine smile that he let quickly slide back off of his face. But I would take it. I would take that smile and know how hard it was to get that from him. I wasn't even sure if he smiled for Mandy. I filed that away to ask her sometime when Trevor wasn't being investigated for murder.

"I need you to help prove that I didn't do it," Trevor said. "Look, I know you don't like me but I know you and Mandy are like family so if you don't do it for me, please do it for her."

I looked out the window at Main Street. If a frozen tundra had a downtown, I'm sure it would look the same as what I could see outside right now. The snow was beating down and even though it was the middle of the day, it was dark and cloudy enough for the streetlights to be on. Everything was covered in ice and snow and it was the kind of day that you could just see how freezing cold it was simply by glancing outside.

The only saving grace was that the Below Zero decorations were also lit up. The buildings were still lined with Christmas lights and the snowflakes on the lampposts were bright and offered a bit of happiness in the cold.

"Okay, I will help you," I said, turning back to

face him. There was an innocent, unabashed happiness in his face that made me feel better about helping him.

"There's only one problem," Trevor said. "I don't really have an alibi. Well I do, but it can't really be corroborated. See, I was at the library studying, but when they closed I left and studied in my car because I didn't want anyone to see me. The cops said they thought Gerald was killed around 7 or 8 that night and I can tell you that I was definitely in my car parked by the lake, by myself, studying at that time."

Well, there was the wrench in the plans. Now I would have to find a way to prove he was innocent without corroborating an alibi of any sort. I guess I could stop by the library and make sure he was there earlier in the afternoon. I'd just have to hope that I actually found something out at the crime scene when Mandy and I ventured out there later this afternoon.

We finished our lunches in silence. Trevor stood up to go, but as he walked by to leave, I grabbed his arm to stop him. He jumped a bit in surprise, which I couldn't blame him for.

"Trevor, it isn't that I don't like you," I said. "I just don't think anyone will ever be good enough for Mandy. But I promise you that I will help you. For Mandy."

"Thank you Tessa," Trevor said with a quick smile. With that, he walked out of the Taco Queen into the cold. I knew that was probably the only time he would say that and I watched his back as he retreated to the apartment he and Mandy shared.

I just couldn't stop getting myself wrapped up in these things, but as hard as it is for me not to blurt out things, it is even harder to say no when my family needs help.

•Chapter Eleven•

My phone rang as I pulled into the driveway and I grabbed it quickly, thinking Mandy may be ready sooner than I thought to go out and investigate. It was quite a surprise when Clark's deep voice came out of the other end. Clark is an incredibly handsome man who didn't grow up in Shady Lake, but moved here to teach social studies at the high school. Despite the fact that he could have his pick of the young women in town, for some reason he chooses to date me, which is an absolute delight to my high school, low self-esteem self.

"Hey Tessa," Clark said. "We need to start planning soon."

I put the car in park and sat for a moment, trying to figure out what he was talking about. All of a sudden, I realized that we had talked about entering the snowman building competition later this week. It all came rushing back through the veil that the murder had put up in my memory.

"You forgot, didn't you," Clark said. I could almost picture his disappointed face on the other end of the phone.

"No, no, no," I said, trying to save face, but it was no use. "Okay, yeah. I have been really busy trying to figure out this whole murder thing."

Winter Festival Murder

"Did the police ask you to help again?" Clark teased. "That Max just can't do it without you, can he?"

Clark and Max both knew that I casually went out with each of them. While they teased each other and enjoyed a friendly rivalry when it came to me, they actually didn't really mind. They both understood that I wanted to casually date instead of settle down, at least for a while. I honestly think that if they hadn't been in a friendly competition over me, that they would be pretty good friends.

"Oh geez Clark," I said. "But we really do need to make some sort of plan. The competition is in two days and we have no idea what we are doing."

"Well, I think the first thing we need to do is decide which direction we are going to go in," Clark said. "Do we want to build a typical snowman shape into something or do we want to make a snow mound shaped like something? I tested the snow this morning and as of right now, it is good rolling snow."

I stifled a laugh because Clark was getting way more serious about this than I had thought. I felt a bit like I was looking behind the curtain of Clark. I knew he was very competitive, but I'm pretty sure there wasn't even a prize for this competition besides a ribbon and some bragging rights.

"Well I think we should do something where we mound the snow, because it is supposed to get colder and I don't think the sticky snow will stay," I said.

Clark mmm-hmmed on the other end of the phone a few times. I could hear him writing something, but I didn't know if that was some ideas for the competition or if he was grading some papers since it was his prep time.

"Good point," he said. "I think the snow mound is our best bet then. Why don't we each come up with three ideas and we will talk tomorrow."

"That sounds good," I said. "We will talk tomorrow."

I got out of the car and shuffled up to the front door. Here's hoping I could actually think of some ideas because right now, the only thing I pictured was a good ole classic three ball snowman. I took my coat off and hung it on a hook in the entry before running into my mother in the living room.

"Tessa, I'm so glad you are here," my mother said. "I need to run to the store real quick. Can you take over desk duty for a little bit?"

"Oh sure," I said. It would give me some time to actually think about this snowman competition so that I wouldn't let Clark down, even if desk duty was utterly boring.

After my mother grabbed her jacket and purse and headed out the door, I made my way to the desk. The desk was an actual desk with a big, old desktop computer on top that ran slower than a turtle. It also had stacks of papers that seemed to perpetually be cluttering the top despite filing and putting them away frequently.

I shook the mouse to wake up the computer and while it thought about it, I got myself a cup of coffee. I wouldn't be able to do much planning without a little liquid inspiration. By the time I got back, it was ready to go. I typed "snow building ideas" into the search engine and hit go.

After wading through some snowman ideas that I thought were too blah for a competition, I found a few cool ideas. I felt a little guilty that I wasn't thinking up the ideas on my own, but I've never been a totally creative person. Give me something to go on, sure. But just thinking of something out of the blue? It just doesn't work for me. I got a piece of paper and wrote down the ideas I had found.

Snowman Ideas

1. Upside Down Snowman

2. Snowdog (or other animal)

3. Thermometer showing below zero

There, I had done my duty and come up with three ideas. And actually, none of them were a cop out. I thought they were all pretty legitimately good ideas. Hopefully Clark and I would be able to agree on one to build. I sat back in my chair and took a breather just as the front door slammed shut.

Winter Festival Murder

Lennie walked inside clutching a few papers in his hands, blown with a flurry of blowing snow and I caught my breath. I wonder if he had been questioned by the police yet. He definitely should have been, after the threats he lobbed at Gerald during the kickoff festival.

"Hello Mr. Mickelson," I said, squinting at the papers in his hand. The only one I could see was too far away to be read, but I recognized the logo for Shady Lake Bank and Trust. "How are you today? It's such a shame that the medallion hunt was thrown so far off track."

Lennie scowled at me as he took his purple and yellow scarf and his leather jacket off and hung them both up. He was a frequent guest and also a frequent grump. Even his excitement about the medallion hunt had been overshadowed by his grumpiness about Gerald being the winner every year.

"It is a shame," he said. "I actually thought I was going to win this year. I knew exactly where the medallion was. Leave it to Gerald to ruin the medallion hunt, even in death."

"You're right, he should have been murdered somewhere unrelated to the hunt," I said before I could stop myself.

Lennie threw a glare my direction and I put on my fake customer service smile to disarm him. After a

Winter Festival Murder

silent stare down, he moved towards the staircase. I wanted to ask him more questions, but I wasn't exactly sure what to ask or even how to ask. So instead, I let him go.

I checked the bed and breakfast register and saw that he was scheduled to stay until the end of week, so maybe I could find another time to ask him a few questions. I had to figure out a better way to approach him about it.

As I sat on desk duty and waited for my mother to come back, I pulled up a card game on the ancient computer. I changed the picture on the back of the digital cards to be a picture of a desert island. It made the snowy day a bit more bearable.

My phone buzzed with a ding and I pulled it out to see Mandy had sent me a message. Honestly, I was also a little proud I had managed to keep my phone from going on silent.

Come pick me up whenever you are ready. Dress warm so we can thoroughly inspect the crime scene area.

I laughed because usually I was the one to demand we sneakily investigate a crime scene. Mandy usually just came with because she loved me and didn't want me to do it by myself. How the tables have turned since Trevor became a suspect.

•Chapter Twelve•

It had only been a few days since the murder, but the police must have felt that they had thoroughly investigated the crime scene because there nothing there to stop us from tromping into the park and looking around. There was no officer guarding the park and besides a bit of police tape that had fallen down into the snow, there was nothing that told us not to be there. Mandy and I walked carefully down the hill, which was still slippery from all of the snow. I showed here where we the body had been. A small patch of the snow in front of the bench was still pink.

"How awful," she said quietly as she sniffed a few times. "But I need to prove that Trevor did not do this."

Mandy did not have a stomach for true crime like I did. I'd tried in the past to recommend some podcasts to her that I really enjoy, but once it got to anything even semi-graphic, she did not want to listen anymore. It was a bit of a bummer that we didn't share that interest, but that was okay.

I grabbed Mandy's purse and opened it up, grabbing out her gum to give her a piece. She gladly took it and started chewing away. I figured it would help calm her down a little bit. I'd read that peppermint could be calming. Maybe that extended to other types of mint.

"Now I'm thinking that there must be somewhere else besides just right here at the bench," I said. "I assume that Gerald came to search for the medallion and whoever killed him was either following him or hiding somewhere to take the medallion from him."

"I think the obvious place would be those trees," Mandy said, pointing to the bank of trees behind the bench.

"Yup, but we need to make sure we don't destroy any evidence that might be there," I said. "So let's tread carefully."

Mandy nodded and we started to slowly walk towards the trees, watching the ground for any evidence that might be helpful. The one perk about investigating a crime scene during the daytime was that we didn't have to figure out how to search while holding a flashlight.

There were bootprints heading towards the trees, but those could just be from the police searching down here. I looked at them, but since they were all very similar, I didn't think any of them were evidence of anything other than an investigation. It appeared that the police had at least searched by the trees so they weren't totally incompetent.

Behind the bench, three pine trees grew close together. Evergreen Park was called Evergreen Park for a reason. The trees were all healthy, adult trees, but none of them were very big. The best part was that as we got closer, they smelled like pine and to someone who loves holidays as much as I do, it smells like Christmas.

"Hey Tessa, do you think this is a clue?" Mandy said, her voice a little muffled.

I looked up from the matching bootprints I had been looking at on the ground and Mandy was already standing in between the pine trees. I could only really see her feet as the rest of her was covered by tree branches. I ducked in between some branches until I was standing in a pocket between the trees with Mandy. It was the sort of place that would be a perfect fort for some children. It would have also been a great hiding place for a killer.

Mandy pointed towards the ground. There was only a very thin layer of snow in between the trees, but Mandy was pointing at a perfect bootprint in the snow. Someone had obviously stood here and it looked like they had stood there for a while.

"I think it is a clue," I said. "It looks like a man's print by the size. Give me your phone and I'll take a few pictures."

Mandy dug her phone out of her purse. My flip phone had a camera, but it did not take very good pictures. If I wanted the police to take this evidence seriously, I would need a good picture to show them.

I also grabbed a stick of gum and tossed it in the snow to show size. I gave myself a little imaginary pat on the back for thinking of that.

As I snapped a few pictures, I noticed something partially buried in the snow next to the bootprint. It looked like someone had dropped it and it had been partially stepped on. I had mittens on, so I wasn't worried about contaminating evidence as I brushed some snow off of it. It was a piece of plastic that had "Loony Bin" printed on it with a picture of a loon. It was a keychain. I wondered if it had fallen off of the killer's key ring. I took a few picture of where I had found it in the snow for posterity.

Trevor spent a lot of time at the Loony Bin. It was the newer bar in town and all of the young townies went there. What if this had fallen off of his key chain? I was about to ask Mandy about it when she spoke first.

"Tessa, do you hear that?" Mandy said. She stood up suddenly, her eyes wide. "I think someone else is here."

I stopped my picture-taking, but I didn't hear anything. I wasn't sure if it was because there was nothing there or because I was too involved in my picture taking. I listened for a moment before I shook my head at her. I didn't hear anything.

"There it is again," she said. "I think someone just parked up in the parking lot."

She was right, I could faintly hear the sounds of a car parking. I hoped it was just someone who lived in the neighborhood coming home, but I wasn't sure. Without thinking too much, I kicked a little snow over the key chain. Not enough to hide it completely, but enough that the police would find it if they actually looked a little bit.

"I'm done taking pictures," I said. "So let's sneak out of here and maybe try to sneak around and up back to the parking lot."

The park sat right next to a residential street. If we could sneak from the trees over to the sidewalk that ran next to the street, we could walk up to our car like we had just parked here so we could take a walk around the neighborhood. It would have been an odd walk on a very cold day, but I was more concerned about someone finding us right next to the crime scene.

We walked out of the trees away from the park bench, careful not to disturb the bootprint or any other evidence that might be there. I would have to figure out how to tell Max about what we had found. I'm sure he would be angry that I'd been snooping around.

As we tried to make our hasty exit, we heard a shout.

"Stop right there," a voice said from the top of the hill.

Winter Festival Murder

We froze for a moment and by the look on Mandy's face, I could tell we were thinking the same thing: the killer had come back and now he was after us. I wasn't sure whether to run or try to hide, but if the killer had already shot someone once I was sure they'd shoot us. There was no point in running.

I searched Mandy's face to try to figure out what we should do. She grabbed my hand and squeezed it. Together, we started to run.

"I said stop," the voice said. "Stay there or else you will be in trouble."

Mandy froze again as I tried to pull her along. That was it. The killer was going to get us. I turned to face who was yelling at us.

Winter Festival Murder

•Chapter Thirteen•

I bravely turned to face my doom and saw that the deep voice who had been yelling at us was, in fact, not the killer, but Officer Max Marcus complete in his uniform. I had been too involved in finding clues that I had failed to recognize the voice as being his. I cringed inward at my own stupidity.

"Stop right there Tessa and Mandy," Max yelled once more.

This time as he descended the hill, he looked a little more dignified than when he had been charging down the hill on a sled, coming to my rescue. He did still have to shuffle sideways down the hill so that he didn't slip and fall down the icy snow so it wasn't totally dignified, but it was better.

I tugged on Mandy's arm and pointed towards Max so she could see that it was just him and not someone trying to kill us. She rolled her eyes and waited with me until Max shuffled to the bottom of the hill and then jogged towards us.

"Tessa, I don't even have to ask what you are doing here," Max said, giving me a disapproving look. "But Mandy, I'm a little disappointed to find you here with her."

Mandy was forever having people think that I drag her into our shenanigans and while that is true sometimes, other times they are definitely her idea. Take today, for instance. She was just too innocent looking to make anyone suspect her. It was just a curse I had to bear, just like as the oldest sibling I was constantly blamed for making my brothers and sisters upset when we were younger.

"Well maybe if you guys would do your job fully we wouldn't have to come out and look on our own," I snapped. It was true. Every time I went to investigate a crime scene, I'd end up finding something they missed. The Shady Lake police seemed to get a little too excited every time they had a big case to solve and they ended up making mistakes.

Max furrowed his eyebrows at me. He couldn't really dispute it because it was true. But I realized that I couldn't make him too mad. He was my link into the information the police have and even though he tried not to tell me anything, I could usually get some information out of him.

"Sorry," I said, in a rather unconvincing way. "But we did find something over there in the trees. Did your guys search in there?"

"I'm sure they glanced in there," Max said. I could tell he was bluffing. If they looked in there, it must have indeed been a glance to not notice the bootprint. And if they found the bootprint, they would have found the keychain too.

"Well we just found a bootprint in there that

you should know about," I said. I was trying to suppress more sassy comebacks because I needed him to tell me about any other clues they found. "And underneath the bootprint was a keychain from the Loony Bin. I did take some pictures, but why don't you just come see it in person."

Mandy and I led the way to the grouping of trees and together we parted the branches so that he could see inside. I was able to analyze the scene a bit more now and it looked like whoever had been in there had come from the tree filled area behind the trees, not immediately from the park.

"See that big bootprint right in the middle?" I said. "That must have been where the killer stood and waited. And they must have dropped that keychain that is buried in there."

Max nodded a few times. He appeared to be deep in thought. He usually tried to keep me out of trouble, so he was probably wondering how to get his guys back down here to look at the new evidence without telling them that I had been the one to lead him there.

"Before I call for another investigator to help me, why don't you guys come up and sit in my warm car and we can chat," Max said.

"I'd rather sit in the station wagon," I said. The squad car only had two seats up front and I didn't feel like it would be fair to ask Mandy to sit in the back

Winter Festival Murder

like a criminal. The station wagon wouldn't be as warm, but at least we'd all be able to talk without a cage between us.

We all walked to the sidewalk and then up the hill to the parking lot so that we didn't have to attempt to climb the slippery hill. I started the station wagon and turned the heater up without putting it on full blast because otherwise we wouldn't be able to hear each other talk over the fan.

I turned down the radio even though Party Line was on right now and someone had just called in to complain about the snowplow drivers. From the portion of the call I caught, the plow driver always plowed the snow into the caller's driveway and this time the caller thought they had gone too far. This time the driver had knocked over the home owner's garbage can and broken it and the city refused to pay for it. Darn, it sounded like I was missing a good one.

"So I'm assuming you are searching because we had Trevor in to be questioned," Max said as he settled into the backseat of the station wagon. The police might not be able to investigate a murder thoroughly, but he was sure able to put the pieces together.

"You bet," Mandy jumped in to say. "Trevor is innocent and we are going to prove that to you."

Max sighed a big sigh from the back seat. I knew what he was thinking, but I waited for him to say it.

"You can't just come barging in to try to investigate," he said. "You are not police officers or even private detectives. Stay out of it."

"No," Mandy said. It was forceful enough that I turned and looked at her in surprise. Mandy was usually the quiet one who never contradicted anyone. Max was surprised as well, as evidenced by his eyebrows which were now high enough on his forehead that they were almost part of his hairline.

"Trevor is innocent and I am going to help prove that," Mandy continued. "I am not going to wait for you all to bumble your way through this thing like usual. No offense Max, but I'd rather not put Trevor's life in the hands of your incompetent department."

We all sat for a minute, taking in what Mandy had said. Mandy was so fired up that there was almost fire shooting out of her eyes towards Max. I knew she loved Trevor, but this level of mama bear was admirable.

"Okay," Max finally said. "That's a fair point."

"Yes it is," Mandy said. "And now, since we showed you the bootprint and the keychain, you are going to tell us about any other evidence you found."

My jaw dropped open. Mandy's level of daring was amazing right now. I usually had to trick Max into telling me things. I sat and waited to see if this would actually work. It was entertaining enough that

Winter Festival Murder

I almost wanted some popcorn to go along with this show.

Max appeared to be thinking about her request. I debated whether I should say anything. Max would be more likely to say something to Mandy, but I already knew a few things about the case since I was the one that found the body.

"What about the gun?" I asked. "Was there any evidence on the gun?"

"We didn't find any fingerprints," he said carefully after giving it some thought. "We didn't think we would since this happened outside and it's been so cold that everyone was likely wearing gloves."

I got the distinct idea that Max was holding something back. The car was finally starting to warm up, so I took my hat and mittens off while I thought about whether to say something to Max or not. If I poked him too hard, I'd just regret it because he would get mad. Mandy might be our only hope at more information and Max seemed like he wanted to say more. I sat and waited to see what Max would reveal.

•Chapter Fourteen•

We sat in the car, each of us waiting for someone else to talk. I reached over and turned the heater down a bit more so that it would be easier to hear each other. It was warm enough now that we didn't need my poor car to work overtime pumping out heat.

Mandy glanced at me, her eyes seemed to ask what she should do. While I frequently came to her for help when I was trying to solve something, she hadn't really been this involved before. The thought of how much she loved Trevor came rushing into my mind again and I tried not to scowl. You know how some people can talk with their eyes? Mandy and I can do that, so I answered her with my eyes and said she needed to take the lead. As always, she understood and gave me a little nod.

"Max, tell us more about the gun," she said. Mandy was so quiet and gentle that I think most people would tell her their deepest, darkest secrets.

Mandy folded her hands in her lap and looked straight at Max. She wasn't staring at him and her facial expression was neutral, but she was exuding an air of 'tell me right now' that I envied her for. I glanced out the window, not wanting to break the spell with my big, dumb facial expressions.

Winter Festival Murder

A very light snow shower was passing and we seemed to be surrounded by falling snow in the station wagon. It felt like we were the only three people in the world right now. Snow was always something that I loved to see. It didn't matter if it snowed on the high school football game, at Christmas time, when it was below zero, or even when it was late in spring. Snow always has a magical quality for me. Right now, it felt like the snow was providing a gentle backdrop to our morbid investigation. I turned back to look at Max as he started to answer.

"Well, there was something a little curious about the gun," Max said carefully. "Obviously there were no fingerprints on it, but there were some fibers by the trigger."

"Fibers?" Mandy said. "What do you mean by fibers?"

I squeezed my mouth shut even though I was dying to ask questions. I just needed to wait this time. Mandy was turning out to be a more shrewd interrogator than I was, despite her quiet nature. Hopefully there wouldn't be a next time for this sort of investigation, but if there was I'd be bringing Mandy along.

Max looked like he wasn't sure whether he should say anything else, but he was slowly lured into Mandy's quiet, unassuming trap. I could see him weighing things back and forth in his head, trying to figure out if telling us would be helpful or not.

"We aren't sure what they are from, but there were purple and yellow fibers on the gun," Max said. "They looked like they were from some sort of outerwear, like mittens, scarves, or a hat. I suppose they could be from a sweater, but it has been so cold that I think anyone wearing a purple and yellow sweater would have a jacket on over it. Gerald wasn't wearing anything with those colors, so we are assuming that they are from the killer."

Purple and yellow fibers. Whoever it was must be a fan of football. Unfortunately, it was the color of the professional football team of Minnesota which meant many, many people wore those colors. It was a helpful tip that also was not helpful.

"Thank you for telling me," Mandy said. She looked Max in the eyes and smiled. "That is an interesting clue to all of this."

Max shrugged and ran his hand through his blond hair. I couldn't help but smile at him. We had grown up since high school but right now he looked like a teenager again, wearing his conflicted emotions on his sleeve. I leaned back to the backseat and gave his hand a squeeze. He squeezed my hand back with a little smile. I was hoping that was a sign that he had forgiven me for my thoughtlessness the other night, but he quickly pulled his hand away as if he had suddenly remembered that he was upset with me. I tried to catch his eye and see if I could send him a silent apology, but Max seemed to be avoiding my gaze.

"I should get back to work," Max said. "I will need to call a few guys to come take a look at that bootprint."

"Thanks Max," I said.

Max gave one more shy smile and climbed out of the car. He walked towards his squad car but before he got in, he turned and waved his hand to tell us to go. He didn't want us to be at the park when the rest of the officers got there.

I didn't really know where we should go. We needed to talk a little about everything we had seen and thought about, but we couldn't go to the B&B where everyone was basically on top of each other. We couldn't go to Mandy's because Trevor would be there.

We drove around the lake in silence a few times. The lake was frozen through and dotted with ice houses. It was a weekday, so there wasn't much happening out there but a few of the houses had a car parked next to them. On the weekends, there would be lots of fishers both in their houses and just next to an open hole. Snowmobiles would be racing back and forth and there might even be a few ice skaters or a pickup hockey game happening out there.

"Why don't we go to the Loony Bin?" Mandy suggested. "We'll be able to grab a small table at the back and be able to talk without too much interruption. Plus, I'm hungry."

On our next go-around the lake, I steered off towards downtown. I was a little disappointed because I would have preferred to get one of Mandy's donuts at the Donut Hut, but I suppose I could get a dessert. Or I could follow Mandy's example and get something healthy for lunch.

•Chapter Fifteen•

We settled ourselves into one of the more private tables at the back of the Loony Bin and soon enough we were tucking into our food. Mandy had ordered a sensible lunch of a salad and a bowl of soup. I ordered a large grilled cheese sandwich with an appetizer of fried mozzarella sticks. After briefly considering a healthier lunch, I had settled on something comforting instead. Winter called for warm, comforting food. I'd save that healthier stuff for warmer weather. Plus, a little self care in the form of melty cheese was in order after realizing that Max was still mad at me.

The Loony Bin was in a bit of a lull right now as it was after lunch but not quite happy hour. Right now Mandy and I were the only customers in the place. Charlie was polishing glasses behind the bar and I assumed Rich was in the kitchen cooking and preparing for happy hour and dinner. That meant it was the perfect time to sit and discuss the investigation.

"I think the next thing we need to do is make a suspect list," I said. I dug in my large purse and pulled out a pen and a pad of paper, which I handed to Mandy. She had neater writing and if I was working with someone else, we would need to be able to read the list instead of using my usual chicken scratch.

At the top, she wrote SUSPECTS and then made three columns, one for names, one for pros and one for cons. Mandy looked at me. I was apparently the lead investigator in this, so I jumped right in and took the lead.

"First we should list the names," I said. "Put Trevor on there. Even though we think he is innocent, the police don't and we have to think like them. Lennie was threatening Gerald at the kickoff ceremony."

Mandy was carefully writing all of the names down. I dropped my voice down to a lower volume.

"Write down Charlie too," I said, trying not to glance over at him. I didn't want him to think I was being suspicious, especially if he was the killer. "He was threatening Gerald also."

"Anyone else?" Mandy said. She started chewing on the end of the pen. If she hadn't been eating lunch, she would have definitely been chomping on a piece of gum instead, but the pen would have to take the brunt of her nervous energy for now.

I racked my brain trying to think if there was anyone else that had been taking the medallion hunt seriously. That was obviously the motive, so who else had been serious about it? Suddenly, one more person popped into my mind.

"Put down Donna Grand," I said, thinking back to our conversation at the royalty coronation. She seemed to be a bit of a stretch as a suspect, but she had been really serious about winning the prize money.

Mandy gave me a questioning look, but wrote her name down in the suspect list.

"Let's start at the top," I said. "Trevor was really into the medallion hunt. And he doesn't really have an alibi."

"But he doesn't own anything purple and yellow," Mandy said quickly, jotting down the pros and the cons.

"Lennie and Charlie both threatened Gerald in front of everyone," I said. "But I think we need to do a bit more looking into them."

"Agreed," Mandy said. "Now what about Donna?"

"Donna told me that she was quite desperate for money," I said. "She said she was working hard for the medallion hunt so she could win the money to help her with the bills."

Mandy looked like she didn't really believe me, but she wrote it down anyways. I understood because Donna looked like she wouldn't hurt a fly. But her passion about winning that prize money seemed to make her a suspect in my eyes.

Winter Festival Murder

Then we tried to think of a few reasons why they wouldn't be the murderer. I assumed that Charlie would be here at the Loony Bin at that time of night. He is the main bartender and seems to spend a lot of his time back behind the bar where he was right this minute. I'd have to figure out a way to make sure he was actually here that night. I would also have to check Lennie's alibi. He stays at the B&B with us, so I'd be able to ask around and see if he had been seen around that night.

The next thing we thought about was motive. While Donna had a motive, it wasn't a very strong one. Killing someone over the $500 reward that came with finding the medallion? That doesn't seem likely. There had to be something else behind it. Plus Donna had a young child. Where had Bobby been if she had been the one out in the middle of the night medallion hunting and murdering?

By the time we were done thinking about our list, happy hour was about to start and the regulars were trickling in as they got off of work. Each time someone came in, the crowd would greet them with loud cheers and energetic waves. When Chelsea came in, she greeted everyone enthusiastically, but managed to still throw a glare my way. I was a bit impressed that she even saw me here at the back. She was able to pick me out of the crowd and make sure I got her disapproving look. She didn't like me to invade the Loony Bin, which she seemed to think was her space.

The Loony Bin had really filled a gap in the social lives of many young Shady Lakers. I can't say I approve of going out drinking every night, but The Loony Bin also provided entertainment in the form of local musical artists, trivia nights and during the warmer months, outside sports. Having a place like this around would certainly help the young people stick around, which had been a problem for a while. I really shouldn't be one to talk, though, since I had left too. I just happened to come back.

I grabbed the list and folded it up, sticking it into my purse. As more and more people came in, I didn't want it to potentially be seen. Besides, I had a sandwich to finish. I had gotten so into the suspect list that my poor grilled cheese was almost cold.

Mandy went back to her salad. She had wisely eaten her soup before it could get cold and now just had her healthy salad left. The only problem was that each time she started to take a bite, someone would call her name from across the bar to say hello. She would wave and I would turn and the person would usually offer me a lukewarm, second hand hello also. That's how it was when you didn't stay and become a townie.

The next time the door opened, Clark was the one who walked in. He technically wasn't from town, but he was greeted like a townie. The rules of who is and who isn't a townie don't really make sense. Clark strode in, smiling and waving at his adoring fans. He must have come straight from school. The women in the bar were especially drawn to him and I couldn't blame them. Clark was literally tall, dark, and handsome. He also had only been in Shady Lake for a few years, which qualified him as new blood, unlike all of the boys we had known since preschool.

He seemed to spot me and give me a little wave of his hand. A wave of grief hit me suddenly as a picture of Peter doing the exact same thing flashed into my mind. Peter and I had spent a lot of time out at trendy bars with our friends. We would frequently meet after work and I always loved the moment when he spotted me across the bar.

Clark slowly made his way to our table, fending off physical affection from the ladies and giving high fives to the men. Chelsea in particular tried to hang on him as he walked by. He gave her a hug, but politely dodged a kiss from her, letting it land on his cheek instead. Chelsea's face flushed red for a moment before she turned back to some other men. She and Clark did date occasionally and as annoyed as it made me, they were free to date each other.

"Well hello there Tessa," he said, his dark eyes flashing as he reached our table. "Hey Mandy."

Winter Festival Murder

"Hi Clark," Mandy said as she tried to finish up her salad before someone else came to greet her.

"Clark, I'm so glad you're here," I said. While I had remembered to come up with ideas for the snow sculpture we were going to make for the competition, I had kind of forgotten to tell him my ideas. "We need to finalize our ideas for tomorrow."

Clark grabbed a chair from a nearby table and pulled it up at the end of our table. He reached over and grabbed a mozzarella stick and gobbled it down, not seeming to care that it was hardly warm anymore.

"I'm not going to lie to you Tessa, I don't have any ideas," Clark said. "I had the best intentions to come up with some, but then I was told that I needed to teach an additional class at school now and so my snowman idea time became lesson planning time."

I smiled at him because for once, I had actually done more work than he had. Usually I was so busy that something like this snowman competition would unfortunately fall by the wayside until I would need to think about it spur of the moment.

"That's okay, Clark," I said. "Because I actually have three ideas. None of them are revolutionary, but they are doable."

Clark smiled at me and I got all giddy inside, but I tried to play it cool. As always, I am not quite sure what Clark sees in me. He could have the pick of any woman in Shady Lake and while he does date others just like I also date Max, somehow he keeps coming back to me. I tend to not have much confidence in myself when it comes to my appearance, but Clark's interest in me does help. It does not help me to be able to put together a cohesive thought sometimes.

As I sat and made goo-goo eyes at Clark, the bar erupted in another cheer of welcome. I tore myself away from Clark's beautiful face and saw that Trevor had walked into the bar. Mandy's eyes lit up and she abandoned the rest of her salad to dash across the bar and run into his arms. I found myself smiling, a real, genuine smile. Ever since Trevor had let me in on his secret studying, I found myself feeling a bit more positive towards him.

I glanced back over the bar to see what others were possibly thinking. I wasn't sure who else knew that Trevor was a suspect and had been questioned by the police in Gerald's murder. No one seemed to think one way or the other.

Except for Charlie, whose face darkened when Trevor stepped through the door.

•Chapter Sixteen•

As Trevor and Mandy made their way towards the bar, the mood seemed to shift a little bit. Things got just a bit quieter. Eyes started to shift around just a bit. It seemed that maybe the other townies did know about the questioning. But Trevor was one of them and they seemed to stand on his side.

Charlie's face was dark and I wasn't sure what he was thinking. Did he know something about Trevor or the murder? I had to get closer so that I could hear him better.

I abruptly stood up and my chair almost fell over before I caught it. Clark gave me a startled look and I felt bad because I had gotten so into what was going to happen between Trevor and Charlie that I kind of forgot he was sitting there.

"I'll be right back," I said, dashing off towards the bar before Clark could do anything besides give me a confused look before grabbing another mozzarella stick.

The crowd around the bar was thick, but I gently pushed my way through, giving a smile to anyone who tried to glare at me. I made my way to the front just as Trevor and Mandy got there from the other side so that I was standing next to Mandy, who gave me a confused look at my sudden appearance.

Apparently her heart eyes for Trevor was totally missing Charlie and the storm that seemed to be brewing.

For a while, Charlie worked around Trevor, taking drink orders from anyone and everyone except for him. Finally, the crowd seemed satisfied for drinks and had floated back a bit to sit at the tables, leaving only Trevor, Mandy, and I pressed up against the bar.

"What do you want?" Charlie growled. He looked straight at Trevor, ignoring Mandy and I.

"I'd just like a beer," Trevor said flatly.

"Yeah? You sure you haven't come round just to ruin something else?" Charlie said. He sounded angry and he was getting louder.

"What are you talking about?" Trevor asked. He looked genuinely confused. I was kind of glad because I certainly didn't know what was going on and I didn't want to be the only one.

"I'm talking about you killing Gerald and ruining the medallion hunt," Charlie snarled.

The bar fell silent and I glanced around. Everyone was doing the thing where they were all listening, but trying very hard to make it look like they weren't listening. So no one was looking at Charlie and Trevor, but they were all listening.

"I didn't kill Gerald," Trevor said. He was talking firmly, which was very out of the norm for the laid-back, former skater boy.

Winter Festival Murder

"Oh sure you didn't," Charlie said. He threw the towel he had over his shoulder down onto the counter forcefully enough to make a loud cracking noise. It made several people jump and anyone who hadn't already been watching, now turned their attention towards the ruckus. "Then why have the police questioned you? I really could have used that prize money. You ruined that for me."

"Me?" Trevor said. "How do we know you aren't the one who killed him so that you could get the medallion and the prize money?"

At this point, they both were yelling at each other and everyone was full-on staring at them. No more Minnesota nice ignoring of the situation here. Mandy looked horrified and I felt terrible for her. I didn't care what the townies thought of me, but her entire life including her business depended on these townspeople. I could tell she was feeling conflicted, torn between standing by the love of her life and making sure to keep her customers.

I reached over and gave Mandy's hand a quick squeeze. She gave me a small, grateful smile. I would always be there for her, no matter what.

My attention turned back towards the two angry men who it seemed would have already been tearing each other to shreds if there hadn't been a bar between them. Charlie looked scary, like the kind of person I was afraid of coming across in the dark. And

Trevor's normally laid-back facial expressions had taken a backseat to a snarl that looked like it belonged on the face of a wolf rather than a skater boy.

"Stop right there," came a deep, serious voice.

Charlie's father, Rich, was striding in from the kitchen. He wasn't as tall as Charlie, but he was still an imposing figure and he was not going to let this foolishness happen in his restaurant, even if it was his own son who was the instigator.

"You both need to stop," Rich said as he came behind the bar to stand next to Charlie. "Getting angry at each other will do nothing to bring the medallion hunt back or solve Gerald's murder. And I know that Gerald wasn't exactly a nice man, but he didn't deserve to die and no matter who did it, it was absolutely the wrong thing to do."

The bar was dead silent as everyone took in Rich's speech. I kind of wanted to applaud because those were my exact thoughts and I just hadn't been able to say them. Charlie and Trevor were both nodding at Rich, but they both still seemed to be seething. Once again, I was grateful for the large, wooden bar that was between the two of them.

"Trevor, I'll get you a drink and you and Mandy can go sit down," Rich said. "Charlie, why don't you go to the kitchen and do inventory so you have a chance to cool down?"

Charlie glared at Trevor for a moment more

before he gave a nod and slowly walked back into the kitchen and out of sight. Rich was probably the only person who could get Charlie to calm down like that and I was grateful he had been at work today to do that.

After Rich got Trevor a beer, the three of us joined Clark back at the table Mandy and I had eaten our late lunch at. We all settled in and drank our drinks, picking at the few cold mozzarella sticks that were left. The four of us sat quietly, everyone taking in what had just happened.

"I'm going to go order us some fresh mozzarella sticks," Clark said when the old order was gone. He stood up and walked over to Rich behind the bar to order another round of the gooey, cheesy appetizer and another round of drinks to go with it. I wasn't one to drink too much. I usually drank too much coffee instead of too much alcohol, but after that fight, I think I could use another glass of wine.

After a few more sips, I realized that Clark and I still hadn't talked about our plan for our snow sculpture for the competition the next day. I told him the three ideas I had come up with and we settled on making a large snow thermometer that showed a below zero temperature. I wasn't really that excited for the competition, but I knew I would have fun building the sculpture with Clark. At this point, Max was already mad at me and I didn't want to anger

Clark too.

The door to the Loony Bin opened again, but this time there were only a smattering of greetings. I turned to see who was coming in. My heart fell into my stomach when I saw that Max had walked through the door, but it wasn't a personal call. He was wearing his full uniform and he looked to be at the Loony Bin for a reason.

•Chapter Seventeen•

The bar went dead silent. It was even quieter than when Charlie and Trevor were having their run-in. Trevor's face drained of color and I didn't blame him. He had already been taken in for questioning once; it was totally feasible that he may be brought in again. It did seem a bit harsh to come to a restaurant and drag him out in front of all of his friends though.

Max slowly scanned the room as he walked in. Trevor wasn't exactly hidden, so I wasn't sure what Max was waiting for. He was walking slowly and casually as he looked around.

The door to the kitchen opened and Charlie walked out with our baskets of mozzarella sticks. Instead of delivering them to us, he scowled and brought them to Rich behind the bar, obviously hoping Rich would be the one to hand deliver them so that he wouldn't have to come over and see Trevor again.

Max's stare had laser focused on Charlie and Max was headed towards where Charlie was standing behind the bar. I needed to hear what was going down. My wine glass had a little bit more than a drink left in it, so I gulped it down and hopped out of my chair.

"Just going to get another drink," I called over

my shoulder as I scurried towards the bar.

Clark looked confused. I know I seemed to be acting a bit more flighty than I normally was. Mandy gave me a little motherly scowl that told me she knew what I was doing and she did not approve. Trevor was just slouched down in his chair, not trying to hide, but also not trying to stand out. He didn't even seem to notice that I was leaving.

I got to the bar just as Max did. I had brought my wineglass with in case I needed some sort of excuse to be standing there, but none of the three men even seemed to notice me.

"Charlie, I need to bring you in to the station," Max said. "You are wanted for questioning in connection with the murder of Gerald Pinkerton. I'm really hoping I can have you come with me quietly otherwise I will have to handcuff you and force you out of here."

Max was not a big man and Charlie loomed over him by quite a bit. I suddenly regretted my decision to put myself in the middle of this situation. Charlie's face was getting red, starting from his neck and spreading upward. He started to clench his fists. He was just about to take a step towards Max when Rich reached out and put a hand on his arm.

"Don't be dumb, son," Rich said. "Just go with him quietly. I will get you a lawyer. Don't say anything until the lawyer comes and don't fight them at all. Not with words and definitely not with fists."

Charlie's eyebrows slowly unfurrowed and he gave his father a quick nod before turning towards Max. He looked at Max for a moment before starting to stride towards the door. Max also gave Rich a nod, completely ignoring me standing right there. It usually wouldn't offend me because I was used to him being distant while he was on duty. But this time it stung a little more because I knew he was still upset with me.

When Charlie got to the door, he stopped and grabbed his jacket from the coat rack. He slipped it on and reached in the pockets. He pulled out a pair of purple and yellow gloves that he pulled onto his hands before he headed out. I filed that detail away for later.

As soon as the door closed, the hum of the bar started back up. I knew that everyone was talking about what just happened. Gossip in a small town spreads fast and I'm sure that everyone here was messaging their friends to tell them what had just happened here.

I realized that I still had my wine glass in my hand, so I turned towards where Rich was standing behind the bar. He was just standing and staring towards the door where Charlie and Max had left. After a beat, he noticed I was standing there.

"Tessa, I can get you a refill if you'd like," Rich

said, grabbing my wine glass. He poured me a generous pour and I realized that Mandy would probably have to drive me home if I finished it. "I've also got your mozzarella sticks here. I'm sorry, they may be a bit cold."

I shrugged at him. Apparently this day was destined to be filled with cold mozzarella sticks. They were still tasty, nonetheless. I grabbed the basket of fried food and was about to bring them to my table when I had a thought. I turned back towards the bar.

"Rich, I have a question for you," I said. "Wouldn't Charlie have a pretty good alibi? I mean, he works here at the bar every night. I'm assuming he was here the night of the murder. Couldn't you all provide an alibi for him pretty easily?"

Rich shuffled his feet a little bit and played with his apron. I could see him biting his lip and trying to decide what to say. He must have decided he could trust me, which would make sense. I had known Rich since I was a child. In fact, it was only very recently that I had started to call him by his first name.

"If I'm honest, Charlie actually hasn't been working here as much as before," Rich said, lowering his voice. "I'm actually not sure where he goes, but he frequently takes time away from the bar. The night of the murder was one of the nights when he wasn't working here."

Winter Festival Murder

I had been under the impression that Charlie had a pretty watertight alibi. Apparently I would have to move him into the forefront of my suspect list because now he had a motive and a large chunk of time to do it in.

"I'm sorry Rich," I said. "I didn't mean to pry. I thought it was going to be helpful."

Rich took two steps towards me and wrapped me in a hug. I couldn't really hug him back because of the wine glass I had in one hand and the basket of cold mozzarella sticks in the other. I managed to use the basket to pat his back twice to show that I'd love to hug him back, but couldn't.

"It'll be alright," I said. "You better go call that lawyer."

Rich stepped back and nodded quickly before scooting to the kitchen to make the call. I turned towards the table to see Mandy and Clark watching me. They both had their eyes narrowed, Clark out of curiosity and Mandy out of disapproval. Trevor was still scrunched down in his chair, nursing his beer.

I set the basket of mozzarella sticks down in the middle of the table before taking my seat again.

"Sorry guys, but I think they are cold again," I said.

"That's alright," Clark said.

Nobody made a move to eat any of the mozzarella sticks. We all sat sipping our drinks and silently turning over what just happened in our minds. I really wanted to share what I'd learned about Charlie with Mandy, but Trevor was still another suspect and Clark wasn't involved in the investigation, so I kept it to myself for now.

After another ten minutes or so, the bar ramped back up to the normal volume and the four of us had started to eat the cold mozzarella sticks and talk about other, non-murdery things like the snowman competition.

I finished the third glass of wine along with some other fried appetizers we ordered from Rich once he came back behind the bar. My head was swimming, but in a way I felt young again. Sometimes being thirty, I feel quite old. But hanging out in a bar with my friends, eating whatever I want and drinking as much as I want made me feel young again.

"Come on Tessa, I'm driving you home," Mandy said. "Trevor, I'll be home soon."

I stood up from my chair and immediately lurched. Clark grabbed hold of me and got me back upright. I was suddenly remembering why I didn't drink very much anymore. When you are twenty, this feeling is amazing and you feel like dancing and taking over the world. When you are thirty, you are fully aware of the headache you will have in the morning and you kind of just want to go to bed.

"Whoa there sailor," Clark said with a sly smile. "I'll help you out to the station wagon."

Trevor took another sip of his beer, sitting alone at the table. As we left, no one got up to take our place with Trevor.

"Come on, someone go sit with the poor man," I shouted out as we got to the front door. The wine was making the words just slip right out of my mouth. "You're all his friends. He needs you right now."

Mandy was shushing me and trying to shove me out the door, but I was happy to see a few of the townies get up and move towards Trevor's table. Sometimes not being able to shut my mouth actually worked out to my advantage.

•Chapter Eighteen•

Clark had managed to stuff me into the station wagon with a quick kiss and a promise to message me in the morning, but not too early. I'd see him tomorrow afternoon for the snow sculpture competition anyways. Mandy didn't drive much, but she did manage to get me and the station wagon back to the B&B.

Mandy helped me up the front steps and in the front door. My father was sitting behind the desk, trying to do something on the ancient desktop with Tank standing next to him. When he saw me, he gave a slight smile but covered it up quickly. I was the one kid out of the family who hadn't really done this before. In high school, Mandy and I were two odd ducks who had spent our time doing nerdy things instead of drinking like the popular kids.

"Thank you Mandy," my father said. "Come on, Tank'll drive you back home. Tessa, you come upstairs and drink some water."

Tank grabbed his jacket and followed Mandy out the door while my father headed upstairs. I stood in the entry watching them pull out of the driveway, thinking about how much love I was surrounded by. My family and Mandy had certainly provided me with a soft place to land in my time of need and they were still helping me out at every turn. I teared up. I had forgotten how sappy alcohol made me.

"Excuse me, can I have a little help please."

I turned to see Lennie standing next to the desk. I walked over, trying very hard not to stumble around. Just what I needed was for a guest to know I was drunk while helping them. The desk chair rolled back a bit as I sat down hard in it.

"Yes, what can I do to help Mr. Mickelson?" I asked, talking slowly and carefully so that I didn't slur my words.

"I was wondering if you could check my room's availability?" Lennie asked. "I am supposed to check out tomorrow, but I'd like to stay through the weekend I think. The Below Zero Festival is turning out to be more fun than I expected."

The room booking computer program we used was still thinking really hard about opening on our ancient computer, so I turned and gave Lennie a curious look.

"Really?" I said before I could stop myself. Liquid courage indeed. "I thought the only thing you would like was the medallion hunt."

"I did enjoy the medallion hunt while it lasted," Lennie said. His face was blank of expression. "But I'd just like to see how everything ends up."

"Ah yes, I'm glad you are finally loosening up a bit Lennie," I said. My brain was telling me to stop talking, but my mouth was still slippery with wine and I couldn't stop the words from falling out. "It is still a bummer that the medallion hunt ended the way it did. What do you feel about that?"

Lennie gave me a curious look. I wanted to read that as suspicious, but I knew that a tipsy girl asking about a murder wasn't something that happened everyday.

"Of course it is a bummer that the medallion hunt ended like that," Lennie said. "But I can't say that Gerald didn't deserve it. I know people don't believe me, but he was a cheat. Somehow, he knew where the medallion was every year. That is how he always found it."

As Lennie talked, he got more and more animated, talking faster and faster. At first, I thought he might be getting angry, but then I couldn't really read his feelings. I wasn't sure if he was actually hard to read or if my liquid wine goggles were impairing me. The computer program still wasn't totally loaded, so I took my chances and figured I would ask Lennie one more question.

"Lennie, where were you on the night of the murder?" I asked.

Lennie stared straight into my eyes with a blank expression. I think if I had been sober, I would have been a little scared, but the wine made me boldly stare right back at him.

Winter Festival Murder

"I was here at the B&B," he said. His eyes bored into me and I stared back, not wanting to be the one to break the eye contact. Even if Lennie wasn't the one who did it, he was the type of man who liked to have his way and even though I worked in customer service, I didn't want to be a pushover. I wasn't going to let him get his way.

A silence fell between us until the computer dinged to tell me that the booking program had finally loaded up. I turned back towards the computer and started clicking through the bookings.

"Okay," I said. My mouth was starting to slow down and the words weren't falling out as easily. Hopefully that meant I wouldn't wake up with a headache tomorrow. "It looks like your room is empty. I can extend your stay for another couple of days if you'd like. Through Sunday?"

"Yeah sure," Lennie said. "Do that for me. I'm going out."

He walked to the door and threw on his jacket. As Lennie walked out the front door, I saw him throw a scarf on as a wave of purple and yellow flew over his shoulder. I had been hoping that the purple and yellow fibers would be a great clue, but apparently everyone had purple and yellow. I still filed it away before turning back to the computer.

I clicked around, extending Lennie's stay and wondering why in the world he would want to stay longer. Of course, he said it was because he liked the Below Zero Festival, but I just couldn't believe that. Lennie wasn't really the type to go hang out with the townspeople at a snowman building competition or something. The program saved the room reservation and I stood up, swaying back and forth a bit as I tried to get my bearings.

"Tessa, are you okay?"

I turned and saw Tilly coming down the stairs. She must have been visiting Mom and Dad for some reason. She looked a bit concerned and I realized that she had probably never seen me tipsy before. Most of my family hadn't because I hadn't really ever had any alcohol until I moved away to college.

"I'm okay," I said. "I just came from the Loony Bin."

Tilly's mouth dropped open, making a large O shape. She looked delighted at the thought of her big sister being tipsy. I think I was a bit of a goody goody, always do the right thing kind of big sister so whenever they saw me as human, it was entertaining for them.

"Why don't I help you upstairs," Tilly said, crossing the room to grab my arm. I was grateful for the steady help as we started up the stairs.

"Thanks so much Queen Blizzard," I said teasing her with a gooey, sweet smile. "What a wonderful Queen you are to help us lowly commoners."

Tilly giggled as I slurred my way through my teasing. We had gotten into our family's private living room where my parents were sitting. They had been watching television until I came in, but that went out the window as I loudly greeted my mother. She looked disapproving, but that may have been more because people saw me stumbling out of the Loony Bin. My father simply rolled his eyes. He had been a bit of a wild child in his youth, so while he didn't judge us when we went out to have a little fun, he didn't exactly like us stumbling back home.

"I'm just going to get Tessa to bed before I go home to get my other children in bed," Tilly said.

"You're such a great mom," I said, which was not just the alcohol talking. "Your kids are so amazing and it is because you are so amazing."

Tilly pushed me into the bathroom with instructions to brush my teeth. She smiled as she did it, obviously still amused. I was glad she wasn't annoyed with me because I certainly wouldn't have the patience to deal with a drunk sibling. I suppose that having children had stretched her patience level.

When I came out of the bathroom, I shuffled to my room to find my bed covers pulled back and my pajamas ready to be put on. Tilly was actually tidying my room, which seemed to be like a motherly compulsion she had picked up. She let me dress myself, sticking around to make sure I could get my pajamas on without tipping over onto my nightstand.

As I climbed into bed, Tilly pulled the covers up to my chin and kissed my forehead. In that moment, I felt so much love pass from her lips that I couldn't help but smile. My broken heart was being healed slowly and things like this brought the wound together just a little bit more. I tried my hardest not to wonder if Max's broken heart was being healed the same way.

I drifted off to sleep with visions of purple and yellow outerwear swirling around with visions of Peter and snow sculptures mixing in.

•Chapter Nineteen•

The junior high football field had been converted into a snowman building competition space. The city had used the snow they plowed on some of the streets to bring to the field to bump up the amount of snow that was available for all of the entrants.

Clark and I pulled up to the parking lot and surveyed the scene. It was only lunchtime, so the children were all in school still. The field was filled with adults which seemed like a funny contradiction since it was a snowman competition, but the children would have their own competition on Saturday when they were out of school. Clark had been lucky enough to get a substitute teacher for the afternoon so that we could enter the competition.

We sat in the car and plotted out where we wanted to make our sculpture. From the parking lot, we had an eagle eye view of the field where people were already starting to set up. There were ten more minutes until the competition actually started, which was just enough time to pick a spot and schlep all of our stuff out there.

After a bit of a conference, we picked a spot out a little further from everyone else, but not too far away from the giant pile of extra snow. We would need to bring a lot of snow for what we were planning. In fact, we had a wheelbarrow in the back of the station wagon for just that purpose.

Clark loaded the wheelbarrow with some buckets and things while I grabbed our bag of supplies. We had some red food coloring and spray bottles to make the temperature part of the thermometer we were making. I'm not sure what our snow sculpture would look like at the end, but I knew we would have some fun.

As I walked through the competitive field, I saw so many people getting ready. Of course Ronald had staked off a large area for himself and he was shuffling around inside the enclosure. When he spotted me, he waved at me enthusiastically.

"Hello Tessa," Ronald called. "I'm making a replica of downtown Shady Lake. I'll be excited to see what you and Clark come up with."

"When the competition is over, we will have to come see," I said.

Ronald smiled and continued to scurry around. I wasn't really sure how he wanted to get that done in the two hours allotted, but I'm sure he would do his best. I knew his grumpy wife Melinda wouldn't be helping, but I figured she was somewhere nearby. She didn't let Ronald get too far away from her during things like this. I just assumed she was sitting in their warm car up in the parking

Winter Festival Murder

lot, scowling down at the masses.

I looked around and saw Rich setting up his area. I gave a shy wave and he gave me a sad smile. I wondered if that meant Charlie was still being held by the police, but I didn't really want to ask him about it. Donna was also happily getting ready with the rest of the radio station crew. I tried to wave to her, but she didn't see me. I was glad to see her look so happy after how upset she had been last time I saw her.

Clark had gone on ahead with the wheelbarrow and he was taking things out at the spot we had agreed on. We only had a few moments to spare, so we just took everything out and got our snow building gloves on our hands.

After a minute, an air horn sounded and we started stacking snow together. Clark took the wheelbarrow to the giant snow pile while I worked on collecting the extra snow in our area and making the basic outline of the thermometer. We first needed a giant rectangle and then we would sculpt the thermometer shape out of the top of it.

We spent the first hour just collecting snow and piling it up. We made a rectangle shape about the size of a loveseat, but only as high as our knees. The second hour, we used a little bit more snow to shape a thermometer shape on the top of the rectangle. Then I got some water and blended it with the red food coloring to spray the thermometer with. Since it was the Below Zero Festival, only the bulb of the thermometer would be colored red.

Clark and I were working so hard that we hardly had any time to talk except for a few times when we stopped to quickly discuss what we were doing. I actually really enjoyed the fact that we were able to work well without speaking. I frequently doubted why Clark would choose me, but working so well together showed me why he may like me. Our personalities just seemed to mesh.

My relationship with Clark was totally different from my relationship with Max. I'd known Max for so long that I already knew almost everything about him. I knew his quirks and likes and dislikes. If we had entered this competition together, we would have worked in an entirely different way.

Clark was different. I had only known Clark for about a year now and I was still learning new things about him all the time. This competition was a great way for me to see Clark under pressure. I was so glad to see that we could work together without getting upset at each other. We even ended up with a pretty good snow sculpture despite the pressure of time.

When there were only five minutes left, we set to tidying up our area. We covered any of the red dye that had gone in the wrong place. Clark gathered up our supplies while I carefully tried to write "Below

Winter Festival Murder

Zero Festival" in the snow above the thermometer.

The final air horn blast sounded and we stepped back, pleased with our work. We weren't supposed to stay by our sculptures because they wanted the judges to judge them somewhat blind, so Clark took my hand and we wandered around to see everyone's sculptures.

Ronald's downtown had actually turned out well. It wasn't quite how I envisioned, but it was a few large rectangles of snow that he had carved into the Used-A-Bit, The Loony Bin, and some other downtown staples. It was simple, but it was obviously a bit of a love letter to Shady Lake. I could see Ronald strutting around, quite proud of his creation. I flashed him a thumbs up and a smile filled his face.

We continued to stroll around. The radio station had done a large, old school record player. It was quite impressive, but there had also been an entire team of people working on it so of course they could get something larger done.

There was also a snow dragon, an upside down snowman, a snow dog, a snow cat, a snow tiger, and a random assortment of plain old snowmen dressed up as various people. Clark and I had a good laugh when we spotted a snowman dressed in a sweater vest. Snow Ronald was looking pretty good, but I was glad to see they hadn't tried to make a Snow

Melinda. That would have been a bit mean.

I spotted Donna again and this time she saw me. I waved at her and she started to walk towards us. This was my chance to ask her a few more questions about the medallion hunt.

"I'll be right back Clark," I said.

Clark nodded and wandered off towards the coffee stand with his hands in his pockets. I knew he would come back with coffee for me also. Part of the reason I'm not sure I could pick between Clark and Max if I was forced to was because they were both just so caring, even though Max was mad at me right now.

But I turned back to Donna, who was only a few feet away now. I needed to make this count.

Winter Festival Murder

•Chapter Twenty•

Donna's face was red from the cold, but it looked more like makeup than frostbite on her face. She smiled a wide smile and I found myself smiling back. After finding her crying in the Donut Hut the other morning, I was glad to see this total turn-around. Donna had the kind of expressive face that made you feel what she was feeling. Today, I couldn't help but feel her elation.

"Tessa!" Donna said. "I just saw your sculpture. You and Clark did a fantastic job on it."

"Oh thanks," I said. "I see the radio station has gone all out on their entry."

"We thought it would be fun," she said. "I was just glad to have something to focus my attention on."

I grabbed Donna's sleeve and pulled her away from the crowd. We walked slowly and close together.

"I'm glad to see you feeling better," I said. "You were pretty upset the last time I saw you."

"Well, you could say that," Donna said. "I heard this morning that the police were arresting Charlie for Gerald's murder. I'm just glad that this whole thing can be put behind us."

I tried not to look surprised, but I hadn't heard that Charlie had been placed under arrest. I would have to talk to Max about that to make sure it was true. Charlie did seem like the obvious choice. He was really angry about Gerald and the medallion hunt, he had no alibi, and he did have those purple and yellow mittens. I still wasn't quite sure that he was the one who had done it, but I guess sometimes it is okay to put my trust in the Shady Lake police.

"Donna, I hope you don't mind me asking you a somewhat personal question," I said.

She looked at me for a second, her face squinched up like she was thinking about it. But after looking around and seeing that no one was in earshot or even paying any attention to us, she nodded her head. She seemed to know what I was going to ask before it even came out of my mouth.

"Did you know Gerald pretty well?"

"I've thought about what I would say about this," Donna said. She started kicking at the snow with her boots. I noticed that she wore large boots that must have been men's size. "And I'm not going to lie to you. Yes, I knew Gerald pretty well. He and I used to date, a while back. We kept it really on the down low while it was happening and it was over almost before it started."

"And he is Bobby's father, right?" I asked.

I held my breath, hoping I hadn't gone too far or been too presumptuous.

"Yes, he was," Donna said quickly. "But don't

tell anyone. We agreed not to say anything about it. He didn't ever really want to be a father and I wanted to be a mother more than anything, so I was okay with him not being involved. But he did say he would help us financially."

We had now wandered over to a park bench. I sat down, glad I was wearing snow pants so that the cold of the bench wouldn't seep through my clothes. Donna sat down next to me.

"But he didn't do that, did he?" I asked.

"He did sometimes," Donna said. "But his head was always filled with dreams. Gerald was always more concerned with things like winning the medallion hunt than he was with holding down a steady job to help me out with his son."

I wasn't sure what else I wanted to ask Donna. She had given me almost all of the information that I had wanted from her. We sat for a little while, silently watching everyone who was milling around the competition space. Everyone was bundled up so much that they looked like little marshmallow men running around. I tried to pick out Clark, but I couldn't find him. I hoped that he wasn't looking for me with that extra cup of coffee.

"There have been some accusations of cheating on Gerald's part," I said. "Do you think that is something he would have done?"

"Yes," Donna said quickly. "Yes, he would have

cheated. For him, it was about winning by any means. He would just see that as part of his strategy. Gerald won so many years in a row that I think it is quite obvious that he must have been cheating."

I really hadn't expected that. I figured Donna would have denied all of the accusations and I would have been left questioning. But I think it would be pretty obvious that whoever murdered Gerald probably found out how he had been cheating. We sat again, this time I wasn't sure what to say to Donna so I was glad when she was the one who spoke up first.

"I did love him," Donna said. "I don't want you to think that Gerald was a bad man. He could be hard to deal with and he could be selfish, but there was still plenty of things there that made me love him. He didn't deserve what happened to him."

"I don't think it matters how good or terrible a person is, nobody deserve to be murdered," I said quietly.

Snow started to fall, just a few flakes here and there. I was glad because the frigid cold of a Minnesota winter was bearable when paired with the magic and beauty of snow.

One of the marshmallow men of the crowd pulled itself away from the sculptures and was heading our way carrying two cups of steaming, hot coffee. Even though I couldn't even see his face, I knew it was good ole Clark.

Winter Festival Murder

"Here you go ladies," he said, handing a cup of coffee to me and to Donna. "Two hot cups of coffee for two hot ladies."

Donna blushed and gave Clark a light slap on the shoulder. Clark could be a bit of a schmoozer, which would be a bad quality in a man if it wasn't so broadly applied. Clark was the kind of man who would sweet talk any lady, but would also help old ladies to their seats with a wink. He wasn't a flirt, just an overly friendly man. Most of the time, I found it absolutely endearing. Except when he did it to Chelsea. Then it was downright annoying because she just rubbed it in my face.

"The judging is almost over," Clark said. "They said they are going to announce the winners in just a few minutes. May I escort you two over to the judge's stand where they will be awarding the prizes?"

Clark stuck out both of his arms and Donna and I each accepted one of them. We strolled through the crowd, laughing and having fun looking at all of the sculptures. When we reached the judge's stand, there was a table with all of the awards laid out on top. The top three prizes each had a trophy and there were plaques for other categories.

Tilly was there as the presenter of the awards. She was all bundled up, but she was wearing her Queen Blizzard tiara on top of her stocking cap. She gave me a little wink when she saw me, but I wasn't sure if she was trying to tell me we had won or if she was just happy to see me upright after my wild night last night.

The plaques were handed out first. The radio station won "Best Sculpture by a Business," so Donna left us to go celebrate with her colleagues. The Snowman Ronald won "Most Creative." Ronald's won "Best Representation of Shady Lake."

Then it came to the overall winners. Third prize went to the snow dog, who came complete with a large snow bowl filled with snow kibble.

"Second prize goes to the below zero thermometer," Tilly read with a big smile on her face.

I squealed and jumped into Clark's arms before we rushed to the stage together to get our trophy from Tilly. She gave me a giant hug after she handed the trophy to Clark.

"Great job!" she whispered in my ear.

I pulled back and laughed. Tilly was obviously trying to stay pretty impartial as she was the official award hander-outer, but I was the only winner she had given a hug to.

Clark and I held up the trophy and he gave me a peck on the lips before we headed back into the crowd with our trophy. We passed a stink-faced Chelsea who had obviously been sent to cover the competition for the newspaper and also obviously did not like the public display of affection that Clark and I had just displayed. I gave her a little smile, trying not to rub it in her face too much.

First prize went to Ronald and his Shady Lake downtown. I'm sure every knew who had made that one, but it was such a wonderful representation of our town and it was done with such love that it had to win first place. He stood on stage with the first place trophy, his face wide with a smile.

"Thank you everyone," Ronald said. He took a small piece of paper out of his pocket. "I had a little speech prepared just in case I won. First, I'd like to thank the judges who did a wonderful job. And I'm not just saying that because I won."

The crowd laughed. Anyone else who tried to say that would have been lying, but we all knew that when Ronald said it, he was sincere.

"Next, I'd like to say that all of my competitors did an amazing job. I am so proud to be the mayor of a town filled with such wonderfully talented people. Everyone give a round of applause to the other competitors please."

The crowd obliged with a loud round of applause. I looked around and smiled, knowing that only here in a place like Shady Lake could the entire crowd be so supportive of something as small as the winner of a local snow sculpture competition.

"Lastly, I'd like to thank my loving wife Melinda who has been here for me every step of the way. From helping me with the design during the planning stages to packing up all of the supplies I would need to make my sculpture to sitting in the car during the entire competition in case I needed moral support. I dedicate this trophy and this win to you, sweetheart."

I scanned the crowd until I found Melinda standing towards the side. Her normally sour face was looking a bit less sour than normal, although I wouldn't have called it a happy expression on anyone else. She didn't acknowledge all of the people looking at her or the smattering of applause she was getting. She just stood and looked more frigid than the temperature.

Ronald made his way through the crowd to stand next to Melinda and only then did she seem to warm, ever so slightly. The crowd started to break up as Chelsea took a few pictures for the newspaper of the winners with our trophies. Clark and I went back to gather up all of our supplies. Each competitor had to help encircle their sculptures with some posts and tape that looked like police tape so that hopefully they would stay intact for as long as possible.

Together, Clark and I put up the barriers around our thermometer and gathered our supplies. As we walked to our car, I saw Donna again. I gave her a little wave and once I made sure no one was looking, I made a zipper motion across my lips to tell her I would keep our secret. She gave me a little smile back.

    I still needed to check with Max to confirm if Charlie had been formally arrested. I'm sure he would be reluctant to tell me, but I needed to know. This entire murder just seemed so odd, but I couldn't put my finger on why. None of the possible motives seemed to make much sense. The clues were not that helpful. Maybe the police had found something to crack it wide open. I'd need to figure out a way to have Max clue me in, no pun intended of course.

Winter Festival Murder

•Chapter Twenty-One•

Clark had some papers he needed to grade, so our celebration dinner had to wait until another time. As soon as we got back to the B&B, he hopped into his car and sped off towards home. He was enough of a gentleman to leave the trophy with me to display in the living room window of the B&B.

My parents were waiting when I opened the front door, clapping and cheering. The results of the competition had been aired on the radio, of course, so they already knew that we had gotten second place. Both my mother and father gave me a big hug. My mother held the trophy while my father helped me clear a space on the top of the small bookshelf that sat below the big bay window. The trophy would be proudly displayed there, at least for a while.

"I'm excited to go out and see your sculpture tomorrow," my father said. The sculpture area would be open for everyone to come see all of the sculptures that had been entered in the competition. Anyone who hadn't been at the competition, including all of the children of Shady Lake, could see them all starting tomorrow.

"Your thermometer sounded wonderful on the radio," my mother said. She beamed in pride.

My parents were wonderful in supporting us

Winter Festival Murder

no matter what it was we were striving to do. Between all five of us, they had supported us in sports, arts and musical concerts. They had even sat out on the porch and cheered us on when we took up hobbies like the pogo stick, jump roping, unicycling, and juggling. They were always supportive, even if they didn't especially enjoy watching our hobby. I can't imagine that watching my brother Teddy pogo stick up and down the sidewalk could have been that exciting.

As we stood back to admire the trophy, the front door slammed and in walked Lennie and his sneer. He hung up his purple scarf and jacket and turned back to sneer at us some more.

"I'm not sure why second place is being celebrated," he said. "It isn't like you won the competition."

"Life isn't all about winning," my father said. He had a way of taking things like this in stride and not just because he wanted to keep a guest of the B&B happy. He had always been one to turn lemons into lemonade.

"Sure it is," Lennie said. "Only losers say life isn't about winning."

He scurried away and up the stairs to his room. Lennie resembled a bit of rat as he whisked himself away from us. My parents and I watched him until we couldn't see him any more.

Winter Festival Murder

"If he didn't want to have fun, why did he extend his stay through the festival?" my mother asked when he was out of sight. "You'd think he would want to leave early instead especially after the medallion hunt ended the way it did."

I had to agree with my mother completely. I still didn't understand why he made me extend his stay.

"I'm surprised he wasn't more upset about the medallion hunt," I said. "By the way, he said he was here when Gerald was murdered which I was a little surprised about. I figured he would be out hunting. But were either of you here to confirm that?"

My mother gave me a grumpy look. She didn't like when I "played police" as she called it. My father on the other hand didn't seem to catch on to that.

"The night Gerald was murdered was the night of the hockey game," my mother said. "And after the game, most of the team came over here for pizza. We had people in and out all night eating pizza and congratulating the team on their win. I don't remember seeing Lennie at all that night."

"Same," my father said. "Lennie was definitely not down here with us. If he somehow was here, he would have had to sneak through the crowd with no one noticing him and up to his room where he sat for the rest of the night."

"Okay, so he doesn't have an alibi," I said.

Winter Festival Murder

My mother gave a sharp exhale which I pretended I didn't hear. Once my mother told me that having adult children was hard because you couldn't be as approving or disapproving about things. You had to just let them live their life and only chime in when asked. And I hadn't asked, but my mother had apparently figured both well-timed exhales and grumpy looks didn't actually count as disapproval.

"Pumpkin, I don't know if you heard, but they arrested Charlie for the murder," my father said.

"I know, I know, but do you think Charlie did it?" I asked.

"Rich said he didn't," my father said. "But of course, he's Charlie's father."

I left the conversation at that because my mother's face was telling me that I really did need to stop now. But as I left them to go up to my room to change my clothes, I thought about Charlie. He did seem an obvious choice for the suspect. He had threatened Gerald in public, in front of nearly the entire town. Charlie also did not have an alibi, at least according to Rich. I'm not sure if I'd be able to actually ask Charlie for his alibi. He also had purple and yellow outerwear and having a Loony Bin keychain would make sense for him.

I changed into a warm sweater and a pair of jeans as I thought about the murder again. I still had a hard time thinking that Charlie's motive was winning the $500 prize. In my mind, if you had a big enough amount of debt to want to kill over money, that amount of prize money would barely put a dent in it.

My phone buzzed and I picked it up to see a message from Max.

Want to meet for some snacks at the Loony Bin? I'd love to treat part of the second place winning snow sculpture team.

I had to laugh at Max's message, but this came at the perfect time. He must not be as mad at me anymore, which felt like I'd just shed ten extra pounds off. Maybe I could talk to Rich a little more while we were there. Plus, if I could get a drink or two into Max, maybe I could get him to tell me a bit more about their investigation. I sent him a message back.

Sure, although I think your premise is a bit shoddy ;) See you there in 20 minutes?

I thought about mentioning the other half of my snowman building team, but that seemed like asking just a bit too much. I really wanted to get back into Max's good graces. It was absolute misery to have him upset with me.

You get here whenever you can. I'm already here.

Well, I'd already changed my clothes so I figured I may as well get going. I zipped downstairs and threw my jacket on to venture back out into the cold. It was hard to want to leave as soon as I got home, but I'd venture out in the cold for Max. And I'd venture out there to talk to Rich. I just hoped Rich would want to talk to me because I needed some information from him.

Winter Festival Murder

•Chapter Twenty-Two•

The Loony Bin was full of people, but then it almost always was. I was impressed with the growing economy of Shady Lake. On the other hand, I wondered if I'd be able to find a time to talk to Rich without other people hearing.

That didn't matter right now. I reminded myself that I was here to hang out with Max, not just to question Rich. And right now, I needed to figure out where Max was sitting.

When I opened the door, I definitely did not get the greeting of a regular, but a few people turned and gave a polite wave. While I didn't really care about being a townie, I did wonder how long I had to live here again to be greeted as a townie by some people.

I wandered in and hoped Max would stand up or call to me or something because I was not confident enough to just wander around the entire bar by myself. But Max saved me and called to me from the end of the bar where he had two barstools and a glass of white wine waiting for me.

"Hi Tessa," Max said. "I'm so glad you could come out to meet me. Sit on down here Ms. Second Place. I've already got a drink for you."

I could tell he had already had a beer by the his

casual manner. I knew that the hard part of being a small town cop is feeling like you are always on duty. Max said it had taken him a long time to be able to relax and feel like a citizen when his work week was done. One way that helped was by having a time to relax, whether that was a movie at home or a drink out at the bar.

"I'm glad I could make it," I said. "I need a bit of relax time too after that competition."

Max had already ordered some french fries and onion rings so after they were delivered, I replayed the snow sculpture competition for him. I told him all about the process and the other sculptures. I told him everything, except for my conversation with Donna of course. That part I kept to myself.

"I can't wait to go down and see it tomorrow," Max said, grabbing my hand. The beer had loosened him up enough to allow him this tiny amount of affection in public and I wasn't going to stop it or complain. Beggars can't be choosers after all.

As we sat and enjoyed our drinks and snacks, I noticed that Rich kept looking over at me. I was getting the impression that he wanted to talk to me as much as I wanted to talk to him. But how could I make that happen? I decided to just focus on Max and see how things played out.

After a bit of small talk, I wondered if I could

ask him about the case. I made sure that Rich wasn't around to hear.

"So how is Charlie doing?" I asked. "I heard he has been put under arrest."

Max's face automatically shifted into more of a serious expression. He hated when I asked him about ongoing cases. But I hadn't asked for any secret information, so after a moment, he took another drink of his beer and answered me.

"He is doing as well as anyone does in jail," Max said with a glance towards Rich. "Charlie is under arrest because he threatened Gerald in public and he can't provide an alibi. He was definitely our top suspect and no one else really came up in our investigation. I mean we questioned Trevor, but it was always Charlie at the top."

"Really?" I said casually. "Because I had a list with a few other people at the top of the suspect list."

Max shot me a look that told me not to go there, but I already had. I wasn't going to drop it now. I figured I could press him just a little more.

"I think there are at least two other possible suspects," I said. "And in my mind, they have not been cleared."

I took a sip of my wine and tried to act casual, but I knew I was walking a thin line. Max had just finished being mad at me and if I pushed Max too far, I would not learn anything new and worse, he would be mad at me again. I hoped that wouldn't happen.

"We did find one other clue that you missed," Max said finally.

My head snapped towards him and I couldn't help but show my surprise. I wondered if I would have found whatever the clue was if Max hadn't interrupted Mandy and I while we were searching. I'm sure I would have.

"What was it?" I blurted out. I knew he wouldn't tell me, but I couldn't help but ask. The scene was pretty bare. What could I have missed?

"I can tell by your face you already know what I'm going to say," Max said, picking up his beer mug. "I can't tell you that."

I harrumphed to myself and drained my wine glass. I thought about ordering another, but I knew I really didn't need another glass. What I needed was to find a way to talk to Rich about Charlie and figure out what clue I had missed that pointed towards Charlie.

"I really should get going," Max said. "If I have any more, I won't be able to drive. And I suspect that we don't have much else to talk about."

I winced a little bit. Max looked like I had hurt him and I cursed myself for pushing too hard. Now he was mad at me again.

"I'm sorry Max," I said. "But Mandy asked me to help her when Trevor was being questioned."

"But we have arrested someone else," Max said. "You don't have to help anymore. We have it under control."

"Do you? Because I don't think you have much of a case against him. In fact, I think you are grasping at straws a bit."

"Come on Tessa," Max said. "Knock it off. Just let me do my job and stop sticking your nose into police business. Sometimes I think you just use me to try to get information so that you can play detective."

My face scrunched up into a snarl before I could stop it. I hadn't asked to solve Gerald's murder, but Mandy needed me to.

"Mandy does so much for me and I can't let her down," I said. I started to open my mouth to explain more to him, but Max started talking first.

"You always think you can solve everyone's problems, but you never seem to be able to solve your own," Max said. "Mandy always helps you because you can never manage to do things for yourself. You take on too much and then panic. When you came back, I hoped you had changed a little bit. But you are still just as immature as ever."

"You shut your mouth," I said, slamming down my wine glass just a little bit too hard. "I might be immature, but you are Mr. High and Mighty Small Town Cop. You think you are so great just because you stayed behind to fight crime in Shady Lake, like

Winter Festival Murder

you're some kind of superhero. Has life turned out the way you planned? Because I don't remember this being your plan."

Max's eyes flared. I had pushed him too far. Now he was past hurt, he was angry. My big mouth had gotten me in trouble again. I wasn't sure how I was an adult if I couldn't even learn to keep my mouth shut, but I just couldn't help it sometimes.

I tried to figure out what to say next, wondering if I should apologize, but Max pushed his chair back and stood up gruffly. He grabbed his jacket off of the back of his chair and threw a couple of crumpled dollars onto the bar.

"You never change, do you Tessa?" Max growled. "You never know when to stop pushing and stop talking. I wish you would just grow up a little."

I watched his back as he walked out of the door and my heart sank. When I was married to Peter, I sometimes wondered if Max was the one that had gotten away, like in all of those romance stories. Sometimes I would play "What If" and think about what my life would be like if I had stayed with Max. I never imagined I'd actually be back in Shady Lake and back with Max.

But now I'd possibly ruined it again. I was my own worst enemy, but the worst part was that I knew it and I still soldiered on messing things up. But I knew that I couldn't mess up investigating a little more. I decided now was my chance to talk to Rich. So I pushed my hurt back and gathered up my strength to go have a little chat.

•Chapter Twenty-Three•

There was a bit of a lull in the bar. Not that it was quiet, but everyone had settled into their evening rhythm at their usual spots. I waited until Rich came down my way and I quietly flagged him down.

"Rich, I was hoping to talk to you about Charlie," I said, trying to be as discrete as possible.

Rich nodded, knowing exactly what I was up to. He knew about my uncanny ability to get all wrapped up in solving crimes that had almost nothing to do with me.

"Give me a few minutes to make sure everyone is good and then we can talk back in my office," Rich said.

I watched him go up and down the bar, topping off a few drinks and talking to the two servers who were bustling around with refills and food baskets. When he walked back towards me, he jerked his head to follow him, so I grabbed my jacket and purse and scurried after him.

In the back of the restaurant, past the kitchen, was a door that had a plaque on it that read OFFICE. When he opened the door, I realized that the plaque was necessary so that people didn't confuse it with the cleaning supply closet which was probably about the same size.

Winter Festival Murder

There was a desk right down the middle of the tiny room. It was almost big enough to touch the door when it was closed, but not quite. Rich was a skinny enough guy that he shuffled around the end of it to his chair. He motioned for me to shuffle around to the other side where I sat in a chair that could only sit in the exact space it was already sitting. Above my head hung shelves that were filled with binders which I assumed held whatever sorts of paperwork you need to keep in a restaurant.

"So you want to talk about Charlie," Rich said. He had his hands folded, but he was tapping his thumbs together as he nervously looked around the room. "What did you want to know?"

"I'm not exactly sure," I said with a nervous laugh. "I'm just not sure that he was the one who did this. Something just doesn't feel right."

"I'm glad to hear you say that," Rich said, his body visibly relaxing. "Obviously I feel the same way. I do have a few things I found that may help."

Rich stuck his long, thin pointer finger in the air and bent down, disappearing under the giant desk. When he reemerged, he was holding a file box which he hefted up onto the desk between us. Rich sat back and motioned towards the box, so I stood up and took the cover off.

Inside were a stack of books from the Shady Lake Public Library and I could see the corners of some papers sticking up from underneath. I gave Rich a puzzled look, but his face stayed passive. I started pulling the books out one by one.

"<u>Make Your Own Second Job: Finding the Side Hustle Right for You, Money Management for Dummies, Paying Off Debt When You Don't Make Much Money,</u>" I read the titles as I stacked them up next to the box. All of the books I pulled out were about money in one way or another.

When I got to the bottom of the books, I found that the stack of papers were a large stack of paper job applications haphazardly thrown into the bottom of the box. As I paged through them, I noticed that they were all from neighboring towns. There was nothing for Shady Lake.

I shuffled through all of them and looked up Rich, who was much more relaxed now as he watched me try to figure out what he was getting at. I flipped through the applications again, this time noticing a sticky note with names of restaurants written on it. A few were crossed off, some were marked with a little plus sign and two had stars next to them. I couldn't tell what any of the markings were for.

"What is all of this?" I asked. I had an inkling of where he was headed, but I wanted to hear him say it.

"I found this box in Charlie's car after he was arrested," Rich said. "I knew something has been going on with Charlie, but I couldn't figure out what. Look at this last thing I found."

Rich held a folded up piece of paper. I opened it up and glanced at it. It was a credit card statement with Charlie's name on it. And by the large, red number, he was in quite a bit of debt that he was seemingly unable to pay.

"So the reason he wanted to win the hunt was for the money," I said. "Well, I hate to say it, but that just adds to his motive, Rich."

"But look at the job applications," Rich said. "That's where he's been disappearing off to. I think he's been trying to get a second job to help pay these off. I just wish he would have told me. I would have helped him."

I nodded, trying to piece all of this information together. The list must be the places he had already applied to. I assumed the ones that were crossed off were a no-go. The other markings might mean places he had turned applications in to and ones where he had interviewed.

"Have you called any of these places?" I asked.

"No, Charlie obviously didn't want to tell me about all of this and I didn't want to break his trust," Rich said.

"I hate to tell you, but the police are pretty convinced Charlie did it," I said, realizing after it came out of my mouth that the fact they had arrested him meant it was pretty obvious they thought he did it. "So if we want to help him, we will have to do a little digging into this."

Rich winced, but I couldn't tell which part hurt more: the fact that the police were certain Charlie did it or the fact that we would have to dig through some of his personal problems to try and help.

"Don't worry Rich, I'll take care of it," I said. I started putting all of the papers and the books back into the box. "Do you mind if I take these things with me?"

Rich shook his head and tossed the credit card statement on top before putting the lid on for me. He looked cautiously hopeful and I told myself I could not let him down. The list of people I was helping just kept getting longer. I needed to keep plowing through all of this and just get to the end of it. Even if Charlie did do it, I needed to know.

"I think my first visit will be the library tomorrow," I said. "It looks like Charlie's been spending some time there."

"I wouldn't know," Rich said with a sad shrug. He had always been one of those guys who never looked his age. It was almost like the wrinkles only appeared when he was worried. Right now, the worry was carving trenches in his face that I wasn't sure would fix themselves. That must happen when your child is accused of murder. "Like I said, he hasn't been talking to me about all of this. Come on, I'll help you go out the back so you don't have to lug that box through the crowd."

Rich opened the door of the office and motioned for me to exit first. I squeezed my way out of the door and waited while Rich did the same, grabbing the box off of the end of the desk before I could. He walked me to the back door of the kitchen. He handed me the box and opened the door, letting in a cold swirl of snow.

I started to shuffle walk out the back door, not wanting to slip and drop the box into the snow. It was windy enough that if I dropped it, I was sure the lid would fall off and the papers would blow away and honestly, I needed all of the evidence I could get right now.

"Hey Rich," I said, turning back towards the door. "Would Charlie have a Loony Bin keyring by chance? Like a little dangly on his keys that said the Loony Bin?"

"Oh sure, I gave them to all of my employees," Rich said. "I ordered a bunch to throw into the prizes on trivia night and I figured I could give them to everyone who works here for free."

I nodded at him and turned back to head to the car.

"Thank you again Tessa," Rich called from the door. I turned and threw him a smile, keeping my tight grip on the lid of the box. "And nice job at the snow sculpture competition."

I had to laugh as I heard the door slam shut. I'd probably have people congratulating me on that snow thermometer for months, until well after the snow melted for the season. I was also assuming I'd see a story about it in the paper tomorrow, most likely with an unflattering picture of myself running alongside it, at least if Chelsea had her way.

•Chapter Twenty-Four•

The Shady Lake Public Library was an unassuming building just off of the main downtown area. It was built into a hill so on one side it only appeared to be one story tall, but from the opposite side, you could see that there were actually three stories. I hadn't actually visited the library since I moved back to Shady Lake.

As a child, I had spent a lot of time in the children's library. The upper level had the adult section and the second floor had the children's section. I used to visit several times a week as a child, taking advantage of all of the different programs and classes that they offered. I had even volunteered there, which meant I had been in charge of stamping the due date in the back of the books when they were checked out back before everything was done by computers.

Even when I was in high school, I still stopped by the library weekly to get a new stack of books. I didn't have as much time to hang out there, but I made time to browse the shelves and chat a little bit with the librarians.

But then I left Shady Lake and felt like I had to almost reinvent myself. I was still Tessa, but I was no longer Shady Lake Tessa. I had morphed into some

Winter Festival Murder

other sort of Tessa who didn't have time to hang out at the library and make small talk. I had to keep up with work and my group of friends and the high standards Peter and I had as an up and coming, stylishly urban couple.

I felt guilty when I moved back because I felt like such a different person and I didn't want people to know. I was embarrassed that I had lost touch with my roots. I was especially embarrassed because I used to have a really great friendship with the head librarian, Miss Jill. Back then, I thought she was just the greatest thing since sliced bread and honestly, I still thought that.

As I walked through the front doors into the library building, I tried to push aside my feelings of guilt. The biggest reason I was there was so that I could ask about Charlie and Trevor. I needed to know about Trevor's alibi and if Charlie had been concerned about his debt for a while. After that, I could search for Miss Jill. My parents had seemed pleased when I asked, assuring me that Miss Jill still worked at the library and always asked for an update about me and my siblings.

I pushed open the doors to the library. The adult library was one big room that was only broken up by furniture. To the left when you walk in is the checkout desk and to the right is the magazine section with a few tables and couches for people to sit at.

Down the middle of the large room was a table of computers. They were smaller and more up to date than I remember the computers being and they seemed to be the only things that had changed in the library. The wall opposite the checkout desk was just a large wall of windows looking out on the lake with some chairs where people could relax and read a book while they took in the beautiful sight. Beyond that, the rest of the library was filled with shelves and shelves of books.

When I was in middle school and finally old enough to check out some books from the adult library, I remember having no sense of how they were organized. I never asked either because I enjoyed the surprises I would get from finding cookbooks in one area and European history books not that far away. I would wander around until something caught my eye, not wanting to limit myself to only the areas I thought I was interested in.

I was about to start strolling around on a book treasure hunt when I spotted Miss Jill behind the checkout desk. She was looking older than the last time I had seen her and her hair had turned from blond to gray, but she seemed to be around the same age as my parents. I was surprised to see her because when I was younger, she had always worked in the children's library. She seemed so out of place in the upstairs library.

Winter Festival Murder

Miss Jill looked up from the computer and smiled at me. I was standing in the entryway, trying to figure out what to do first when a look of instant recognition spreading across her face.

"Tessa Schmidt?" she said, phrasing it like a question but I knew she wasn't looking for an answer. "I'm so glad you finally came in. I've been waiting for you."

I walked closer to the desk. Miss Jill was just as kind as she had always been and I felt silly for having been embarrassed. She wasn't chastising for my long absence, but seemed elated it had come to an end.

"Hello Miss Jill," I said. "I'm sorry it took me so long to come in."

"You can just call me Jill now," she said, smiling at me with a wink. "And you don't have to be sorry. I know everything you've been through. It is hard to adjust to a new routine. What brings you here today?"

"I thought you worked in the children's library?" I asked. "I have a few questions for someone who works up here."

"Well then you can talk to me," Miss Jill said with a twinkly laugh. "Once I started getting old, I knew I wouldn't be able to keep up with the kids, so I moved up here and we hired a new, spry young lady to work downstairs. Are you going to ask about a book?"

Winter Festival Murder

I paused, biting my lip. Would I seem gossipy if I asked her about Trevor and Charlie? Miss Jill had been like a mentor to me and I didn't want to let her down by flouncing in and demanding she gossip about townsfolk. I looked around the library while I thought, hoping she would think I was just surveying the library.

"Are you here to ask about the murder?" Miss Jill said, dropping her voice to a whisper. She wiggled her eyebrows at me conspiratorially and somehow I just knew I could trust her. Maybe she'd have to be my Mandy right now since I couldn't talk to Mandy about Trevor being a suspect again.

"Yes, actually, and if you are willing, I could really use your help," I said.

"I can take my break now," she said. "Stay here and I'll go get someone to watch the desk."

Miss Jill walked away and came back a moment later. She grabbed a small coin purse from under the desk and beckoned me to followed her. Together we walked out of the library and down a hallway that lead away from the library until we reached a little alcove with some vending machines that looked like they had been there for decades.

"Here's a dollar," Miss Jill said, taking four quarters out of the small beaded bag and pressing them into my hand. "Get yourself a snack."

I was going to refuse, but she gave me a look

Winter Festival Murder

that told me I shouldn't even dare to try it. As I watched her get her own quarters out, I wondered where that look came from. It seemed to be naturally bestowed on mothers and teachers alike, but it had never been doled out to me. It was a bit of a bummer because it would really come in handy sometimes when I was questioning people about murder.

Miss Jill's snacks fell into the bottom drawer of the vending machine and I smiled as she pulled a bag of gummy fruit snacks out. As I put my quarters in, she stepped to the ancient pop machine next to it and got a can of root beer to go with her gummies. I picked out a salty snack mix and pushed the corresponding buttons. The bag dropped down and after I grabbed it, we walked back out to the windows overlooking the lake. Whoever designed this building did a great job of making sure to take advantage of the view of the lake.

I squeezed open the top of my bag of snack mix while Miss Jill opened her can of pop. We ate in silence for a moment while we watched some snow gently fall.

"So what did you come here to ask me?" Miss Jill asked.

"I actually have two different people to ask you about," I said, wiping the crumbs from my hands on my pants. "First, I wanted to confirm part of Trevor's alibi. He said he was here studying until the library closed."

"He definitely was," Miss Jill said as she popped another fruit snack in her mouth. "He has been in here every afternoon for a month studying. I've been helping him by finding more resources and grading his practice tests. Trevor has come to a point in his life where he has realized he wants something more. He doesn't want to just work as a dispatcher for forty years before he retires. He wants a different job and a family."

I started to think about Trevor and Mandy starting a family. I wondered if Mandy knew about that or if Trevor was waiting to tell her about that too. I stuck my hand back in the bag and realized I had eaten all of the crackers inside. The bag still had some crumbs in the bottom, so I put the corner up to my mouth and dumped it in, only thinking after the fact about how gross that must be for Miss Jill to watch an adult do.

"Wow, I didn't know Trevor had that much ambition," I said.

"I don't think Trevor knew either," Miss Jill said, her eyes shining. "So who was the other person you wanted to ask about?"

"Charlie," I said. "I have some of his library books in my car and they were all about money. Did you help him with that at all?"

Miss Jill sighed and turned back to the

window. As she took a sip from her pop can, I could tell she was weighing something back and forth in her mind. I willed myself to stay quiet.

"I did help him," she finally said. "The poor boy has quite a bit of debt and I gather that nobody really knew why. But he did confide in me and I'm going to tell you because I think it may change how you perceive him. Two years back Charlie was dating a girl from out of town. He decided to propose to her, so he bought a ridiculously big diamond ring for her. The girl took the ring and skipped town and Charlie was left in debt and broken hearted."

I had been under the impression that Charlie's debt was due to bad decisions and while the gigantic ring obviously hadn't been a great choice, it did make me feel for him a bit more.

"No one knows about it," Miss Jill said. She crumpled up her empty fruit snack bag and threw it into the trashcan sitting close by her chair. "Charlie was obviously embarrassed, but Rich was just about to open the Loony Bin and needed Charlie's help. So Charlie took the job even though it wasn't particularly well paying. He never told his father because he didn't want Rich to feel bad for him and his situation and he knew his father couldn't afford to hire too many people. So poor Charlie was stuck."

What a terrible situation to be in. Stuck between familial duty and a rocky financial situation would not be a fun place to be. I understand now why Charlie was so antsy and why the money from the medallion hunt would have meant so much to him. It wouldn't have paid off his debt by a long shot, but it would have been a good sized payment.

"I do think there is something else I should tell you," Miss Jill said, so quietly I almost couldn't hear her. She took a look around, but we were the only people around. "I know how Gerald was cheating."

Winter Festival Murder

•Chapter Twenty-Five•

I gulped hard. Maybe I had misheard her. I knew that Gerald always won and I had obviously heard the accusations that he was cheating, but there had never been any proof. Miss Jill took another sip of her root beer, her brown eyes searching my face.

"You know how Gerald was cheating?" I said slowly, assuming I had misheard and she would correct me, but she nodded back at me.

"I do know," she said. "And I'm sorry I didn't turn him in, but the prize money used to be so small that I didn't think it was worth a hullabaloo."

"So how did he do it?" I asked.

"Do you remember Hilda Foley?" Miss Jill asked. "She used to work here at the library and even after she retired, she still came here everyday to work on writing poetry and stories."

I certainly remembered Hilda because she was hard to forget. Hilda was a tiny old woman who wore her long white hair braided in a gigantic bun on the top of her head. She wore the most colorful outfits that were somehow dated and classic all at once. You would think she had a giant, extroverted personality to match, but instead she was soft-spoken and seemed to let her appearance do the talking.

"Hilda used to write the clues for the medallion

Winter Festival Murder

hunt," Miss Jill continued. "You weren't around, but the clues used to be very poetic and tricky to boot. Now they are, well, I'll call them functional clues."

"Why isn't Hilda writing them anymore?"

"Hilda passed away last summer," Miss Jill said. She had a polite sort of smile on her face, but her eyes were sad. "She was 98 and had lived a long, full life, so it wasn't a surprise, but I do miss her an awful lot."

A wave of sadness washed over me as I thought about Peter and how his life had been cut so short. The grief seemed to come at unexpected times. I had imagined Peter and I growing old together and I couldn't help but wonder how long Peter would have lived without the accident.

My breath caught in my throat as I willed myself not to cry. A warm, wrinkled hand gave my hand a squeeze as I shut my eyes.

"It looks like you are missing someone also," Miss Jill said quietly. I couldn't open my eyes to look at her because I knew that if I did, the tears would come spilling out. "I know what it's like to lose a husband at a young age. It doesn't get easier, but it does become different."

I tried to answer, but it was like I forgot how to make words. I had so many thoughts running through my head at once that it felt like a traffic jam in there.

Winter Festival Murder

"Before I started working here at the library, I was married to Frank," Miss Jill said. "I lost him the same way you lost your Peter. And I still miss him every single day. But the further I get from the accident, the more precious the memories I have with him become. It gets easier and easier to look back on the memories with joy instead of sadness. And I'm here to tell you that it will work the same way with you."

The tears that had been threatening to overflow broke through my eyelids and started to stream down my face. Miss Jill took a tissue out of her pocket and handed it to me before putting her arm around my shoulders and giving a quick squeeze. Only someone who had been in the same position as me can understand. I took great comfort in her words, hoping one day I'd be able to pass them along to someone else in need of them.

"Thank you," I finally said when I had reached the point of once again being able to talk. I dried the rest of my tears, but shoved the torn tissue in my pocket in case they started to flow again.

Miss Jill checked her watch and started to get up from the bench.

"Hold on," I said as I caught her by the wrist. "You never finished saying how you knew Gerald had been cheating."

Miss Jill laughed the sort of laugh that people

usually said sounded like bells before she plopped back down next to me.

"Never get old, Tessa," she said. "Sometimes I stand up and only get a few steps before I forget what I was going to get. You're right, though. It isn't a very exciting story. Gerald found out that Hilda was the one who wrote the clues and while she tried to be protective of them, she liked to take a good stroll around when she was feeling stuck with a rhyme. Of course she would leave the clues on the table and I would find Gerald sneaking a peek at them while Hilda made her way through the nonfiction section at the back wall."

"That's a much less exciting story than I thought it would be," I said with a laugh.

"You still might find an exciting one though," Miss Jill said. "Hilda didn't write the clues this year. So how did Gerald figure it out? Not to speak ill of the dead, but he seemed a bit too busy hurtling through the medallion hunt to actually slow down and try to search it out the old fashioned way."

That was true. How did he end up at the medallion hiding spot this time? I was getting the impression that he wouldn't have done what he was supposed to do and try to actually solve the clues. And I know Max wouldn't have left the clues out on a table for Gerald to find. I also know Max wouldn't have let anyone see him actually hide the medallion.

Winter Festival Murder

This was a case of two steps forward, one step back.

"You've certainly given me some things to think about and you need to get back to work," I said, standing up next to Miss Jill.

"Yes, that's true," she said.

We walked together until we got to the doors back into the adult library. Miss Jill put her hands on my shoulders and turned me to face her.

"Tessa, I know what you are going through and I know how hard it is," she said. "If you ever need to talk or cry to someone who actually understands, please don't hesitate to call me. I don't have a cell phone, but I am listed in the phone book."

I nodded at her, knowing I couldn't say anything to her without starting to cry again. She understood and gave me a quick hug before she disappeared into the double doors of the library.

Once I was in the station wagon, I ran over everything I had learned. Trevor had actually been studying hard and his partial alibi checked out. Charlie's financial trouble was causing him to try and balance money and family. And Gerald had actually been a cheater, even if I wasn't sure what had happened this year.

It had been an eventful day, but I thought back to yesterday when Max had said I missed a clue at the crime scene. It was driving me nuts to not know and while I briefly wondered if he was just lying to get my goat, I knew that he wouldn't do that to me.

Then it came to me: I needed to talk to Trevor. No matter how hard I had searched, so far I hadn't found a reason not to trust him. I would have to get past my irrational dislike of the man child and see him for who he is now. Where he used to be an irresponsible layabout, Trevor was now a man who wanted to better his life. I couldn't argue with that.

Trevor was also a man who not only worked closely with police, but also happened to be good friends with many of them also. I got out my phone and sent Trevor a message that I wanted to meet soon. Maybe he could clear things up for me a bit.

•Chapter Twenty-Six•

Trevor sat on the living room sofa in the B&B patiently watching the birds at the bird feeder. If he was suspicious of me inviting him here, he didn't show it at all. I sat in the armchair next to the sofa, studying him as if there would suddenly be a definite sign whether to trust him or not. No neon light flashed on proclaiming it, so I decided to go with my gut.

"Let's cut to the chase, Trevor," I said. "Max told me that there is a clue I don't know about that they found at the crime scene. Do you know what it is?"

Trevor turned and stared at me with his dumb, blank expression. I had a brief thought that I had a hard time believing he wanted to go to college, but I stopped and gave myself a reminder to play nice.

"First, I'll remind you that I was technically a suspect for this murder," Trevor said. "So they haven't been telling me much of anything, even my friends."

I slumped back into my chair before I realized I shouldn't let him see me be so disappointed. It's hard to keep the upper hand when you keep showing it to everyone. But I was more disappointed in myself for not realizing that.

"But I do happen to know what the clue is," he

said.

My head snapped so hard to the side that I almost gave myself whiplash. Trevor was staring out the window, looking rather pleased with himself. He had a sly little smile on his face and I knew it wasn't because he thought the chickadees on the bird feeder were adorable.

Normally, this sort of look would have prompted me to want to slap the smile off of his face, but it was a bit different this time. This time I was just happy that he seemed to have the information I needed.

"Can you tell me what it is?" I asked. "It'll help me figure out who actually murdered Gerald and it will help clear your name also."

Trevor blushed and looked away. He started to jiggle his legs. Instantly, I got annoyed with him. I was trying to help him and he apparently didn't want to give me information that I needed and that he had assured me he knew about?

"Come on, I need to know what it is if I'm going to help," I said. It came out almost like a gruff growl and I realized I needed to rein myself in if I actually wanted to help him.

"Okay, but it's a little embarrassing because they tried to use it to implicate me also," Trevor said. "The police found a piece of paper in the parking lot. It had gotten wet, so it was mostly unreadable, but they could see that it was from Shady Lake Bank and Trust and whoever it was addressed to owed a substantial amount of money that the bank wanted."

Shady Lake Bank and Trust. That was the bank that Charlie's maxed out credit card had been issued from. Things were not looking good for him, but my gut still couldn't wrap my mind around him being the killer.

Trevor stopped and stared down at his hands. He was starting to blush and the longer I looked at his face, the further up it spread. The annoyance that had been spreading was now being stuffed back down and now I couldn't help but feel bad for him. I wondered if I should ask him more about it, but while I debated that with myself, Trevor kept talking.

"I have received a letter close to that before," Trevor said quietly. "My parents don't make the best money decisions and the bank has tried to come after me before. Thankfully I'm a bit more responsible than my mom and dad and I was able to bail them out. But that happened over a year ago and they've been trying really hard to do better with money."

"So was it your letter?" I asked. I realized that I had neglected to offer Trevor a drink which meant that I had nothing to occupy my hands. I awkwardly folded them in my lap, hoping Trevor wouldn't notice my hosting faux pas.

"At first, I thought it might have been," Trevor

said. "I've studied in that parking lot before and I guess it would have been possible for something to fall out of my car door when I'd open it to throw some trash in a trash can or on a nicer day I would get out and take a stroll when I needed a mental break."

"And you were nervous when the cops showed you the part of the letter?" I pushed gently.

"Yeah, but not because I did it," he said, putting his hands up in defense. "I worried that they thought it was enough to tie me to the crime scene. Obviously it wasn't because they ended up letting me go. After, I went home and saw that my copy of the letter like that was still in one of my financial files in my apartment."

I nodded. It was pretty thin to try and use the letter to implicate Trevor. I was also sure that the police had checked into Charlie's financial history and see that he most likely received a similar letter due to his situation.

We sat in silence for a few minutes, neither of us sure what to say next. I didn't want to break Rich's trust and tell Trevor about Charlie's situation. Trevor understandably didn't want to talk about his financial situation, although I had to admit to myself that I was somewhat impressed that he was so financially competent. I think I've been closing my eyes to the responsible things Trevor actually does and focusing on his immature side which to his credit, has been shrinking with each passing year.

"I should go," Trevor said, standing up from the couch. "Miss Jill is going to help me take a practice test today."

"When are you going to be done with the practice tests and take a real one?" I asked as I followed him out to the entryway.

"Well Miss Jill said I could have been ready months ago, but I'm not sure my confidence was ready until now," he admitted as he shrugged on his jacket.

"Good luck," I said as he walked out the door. "You can do it."

Trevor turned and waved, a shy smile dancing across his face. I hoped that he would tell Mandy soon because if I started to be approving of him, Mandy would want to know what happened and I really didn't want to lie to her about it. Hopefully Trevor would take his test and pass it so he could surprise Mandy with his plan to go to college.

As I shut the door and headed back upstairs, I couldn't help but feel a bit discouraged. This was not looking good for Charlie. I'm not sure how I was going to help him, short of finding the actual killer.

•Chapter Twenty-Seven•

Once again I found myself eating a snack with Miss Jill as we looked out at the snow-covered lake. This time, I had stopped to buy some donuts from the Donut Hut to bring with me to balance out the bad news. I had just gotten done telling Miss Jill all about the bank letter that the police had.

"I agree that it really doesn't look good for Charlie," Miss Jill said before taking another bite of her pink frosted donut.

I popped the last bite of my long john donut into my mouth and licked the snowflake shaped sprinkles off of my fingers. I felt a little bad about stopping for donuts because Mandy was normally the person I confided everything to, but I couldn't say anything about Trevor. She tried to talk about the case, but I shrugged it off. Mandy had looked so hurt as I paid for my donuts and left that it was hard for me not to cry in the station wagon as I drove the short distance to the library. I promised myself that I would text Mandy to hang out sometime soon so that we could catch up.

"What do you think?" Miss Jill said. She looked at me with a blank expression so that I could answer without being influenced by her. I tried to search her face a little for a hint, but there was nothing there for me to go on.

"I hate to say it, but I'm coming around to the fact that the police may be right this time," I said. "My gut says it wasn't Charlie, but everything I find out seems to point at him."

"I will say, I'm all about listening to your gut," Miss Jill said. "I've found that your gut is usually the part of you that takes in all of the information and can process it without anything getting in the way."

I nodded as I thought about it. Thinking with your head means that things you think are fact get in the way. Thinking with your heart means your emotions get in the way. But thinking with your gut doesn't involved facts or emotions. It runs fully on instinct.

"I'm not sure what to do about it though," I said. "Sure my gut may think Charlie is innocent, but I just can't seem to find anything to actually help him."

Miss Jill finished the last bite of her donut. Somehow she managed to make eating a donut look somewhat classy and I hoped that one day I could be like her. It would probably help if I didn't inhale sweets like my life depended on it.

"I'm not sure what to tell you Tessa," Miss Jill said. "But I will say that if your gut is really telling you that Charlie is innocent, you need to keep trying."

I agreed with her, but I couldn't help but feel

frustrated. What else was I supposed to do? I kept looking for clues with little success and I'd even made Max mad in my pursuit of justice. I didn't want to be alienating loved ones and pushing my other responsibilities to the side over it.

"Thank you for the donut," Miss Jill said as she stood up and threw her napkin away. "And I appreciate you coming to see me again. You know I'll always help you as much as I can, Tessa. I'm so glad you came back to the library after so long."

I smiled at her as she was swallowed up by the swinging wooden doors that led into the adult library. There was one more donut left in the box and I couldn't help but take it out and take a bite while I enjoyed the view of the frozen lake. It was another long john, but this one said *Winter* in white icing on the top. I know that Mandy had put it in because she knew I loved seasonally decorated things, especially when they were things that were sweet and not at all good for me to eat.

"Tessa, may I sit down here?"

I turned and saw Donna standing next to the bench. I scooted myself over to the side of the bench again.

"Sure thing," I said, trying to quickly chew and swallow the bite of donut in my mouth. "I'm sorry, but the only donut I have left is one I just took a big bite of."

"Oh that's okay," Donna said, waving away my donut box. "I'm not hungry. I just saw you sitting all by yourself and I wanted to see how you were doing."

"I'm just fine" I said as she sat down. "I should really be asking you how you are doing."

Donna sighed as she stared out the window. I thought about taking another bite of that donut, but I knew that would be very rude. The closed box sat next to me and I knew that whenever I left the library, I'd be gobbling down that donut in the car.

"I'm doing better than than before," Donna said. "Gerald's death was a big shock and I'm not sure I'll get over it for a while."

"Speaking from experience, you won't," I said quietly. My conversation with Max slammed back into my mind as I found myself on the other side of the equation now. Visions of Peter were rushing through my head and I felt the sadness rushing over me.

Donna's eyes got big and her mouth dropped open. She quietly stammered a few times before she actually put a few words together.

"I'm sorry, Tessa," she said. Her face went slack and her entire body seemed to droop. "It was insensitive of me to not think before I spoke."

"Oh no Donna, you don't have to apologize," I said, trying not to gulp for air through the grief. "I know what it is like to be lost in the fog of grief."

Donna sniffed and I turned to see that she was starting to cry. I handed a napkin over to her and tried not to stare at her as she used it to dry her eyes and blow her nose. There have been times where I've been stuck in that loop of not wanting to cry in public, but not being able to stop. The worst part of it is when people sit and stare, even if they are not doing it in a bad way.

"It is just a really weird time for me," Donna said. "Gerald was not a great partner or a great father. We weren't even together when he died, but I still feel like I lost a partner. I actually saw him that night before he died."

This was something I hadn't heard before. I pushed the sadness down as much as possible so that I could focus on this conversation. My fists clenched anxiously, wondering if Donna was going to admit she was the killer. I shook my head slightly because that couldn't possibly be right.

"I met up with him that evening, asking him to contribute to Bobby a little more financially," she continued. "Of course, he scoffed at that which I totally expected. He didn't want to be a father and when he was in a bad mood, he didn't want to do anything to help. And he was in a bad mood that night. I think this year was the first time that he didn't actually know where to look for the medallion."

That would fit with what I knew about Gerald

cheating by pre-reading the clues. This year he probably wasn't sure how to get a leg up on the competition with Hilda being gone. Max had been the one to write the clues this year and Gerald wasn't stupid enough to try and steal them from a cop.

"I'm sorry, I didn't mean to drag down the mood," Donna said. "I actually should be going so that I can pick Bobby up at school."

She stood up and whisked out of the library doors. As the cold draft whooshed in from the door as it closed, I grabbed the other donut and munched on it. Technically I hadn't gotten an alibi from Donna, but I mentally checked her off of my suspect list. She seemed too broken up about Gerald's death to have done it. That meant I only had two other suspects and Trevor left. And unfortunately, most things were still pointing towards Charlie.

•Chapter Twenty-Eight•

When I arrived back at the B&B, I took over desk duty. I felt a little guilty that my parents had taken on the brunt of the work while I was running around building snow sculptures and trying to play detective. I settled myself into the desk chair and prepared myself for a boring afternoon of podcasts and card games on the computer.

I was just getting into a podcast episode about a serial killer when the front door slammed open and a cold wind blew into the entryway. Thankfully we kept a blanket on the back of the chair for this exact reason and I grabbed it to wrap around my shoulders.

Lennie came blowing in along with a swirl of snow and started to take his jacket off. He looked grumpy as ever and once he took his jacket off, he turned to face me. His ever present scowl seemed even more pronounced today and I wondered if I dared say anything, but Lennie actually spoke first.

"I haven't seen you around lately," Lennie said.

"I've been a bit busy," I said. "You may have seen that I won second place in the snow sculpture competition."

Lennie frowned and I briefly wondered if he had any friends in this entire world with that constant expression living on his face.

Winter Festival Murder

"Yes, I saw that terrible picture of you with your eyes closed on the front page of the paper."

I silently cursed Chelsea and wondered how in the world she had gotten that picture on the front page. In the picture, all of us winners were on stage with our trophies and everyone was smiling except me. I don't know what I was doing, but my eyes were closed and I looked like I had suddenly forgotten where I was. Chelsea must have somehow tricked them into running it.

"Either way, I've been busy with the festival and I've also been trying to help out my friend by looking into Gerald's murder. A friend of mine was accused and I wanted to make sure he wasn't arrested for something he didn't do."

"It sounds like you need to butt out," Lennie said, sounding a lot like Max. "You should just let the police do their work."

"I would do that if the police would actually do their work," I said. "They have another person in custody and I'm not sure he was the one who did it either."

Lennie's eyes narrowed and he searched my face. After a few moments, his eyes opened and his eyebrows knit together in confusion.

"So you don't think Charlie did it either?"

"No, it just doesn't make sense," I said. "I mean, I understand how the police are connecting the evidence to him, but I don't think they are right."

Lennie bit his lip and nodded at me. For some reason, I felt like I had to justify my answer to him, so I kept blabbering on.

"I mean, the bootprint was pretty big so as long as he had about the right sized foot, it could be his. The fibers they found on the gun were purple and yellow and Charlie definitely wasn't the only football fan. I mean, even your scarf has the right colors. And the Loony Bin keychain could obviously be connected to Charlie. But the last clue is the one that I think is pretty thin even if the police don't."

"What was the last clue?" Lennie asked. As I blathered on like an idiot, Lennie had been slowly moving closer towards the desk until I looked up and realized he was almost pressed against the opposite side of it. I sat back, feeling a bit uncomfortable with him in my personal bubble.

"It was apparently what looked like a form letter from Shady Lake Bank and Trust demanding a large payment from someone, but the letter had been sitting in the wet snow for so long that it was almost unreadable," I said. Why was I telling Lennie all of this? My blabbermouth was getting the best of me today, but I just felt like I had to justify myself to him. Maybe I was just justifying myself to myself.

"Very interesting," Lennie said. He looked me directly in the eyes, studying me. There was something I couldn't read about his expression and it was making me feel uneasy. It was almost like he knew something that I didn't and it pleased him to have one up on me.

I waited for him to make a move towards the stairs, but he continued standing way too close to the desk instead. I wasn't sure what he wanted since he wasn't usually one for conversation. I wondered if I should just turn my podcast back on, but I decided that was just a bit too rude, even for me. So I sat and stared at him while he stood and stared at me. A Minnesota show-down.

"Did you need something else?" I finally asked.

"Yes, actually," Lennie said. "I assume you are going to go snowshoe tomorrow at the Festival?"

I actually had been so invested in solving this case that I had forgotten about the rest of the festivities. Tomorrow morning, Max would be leading a snowshoe hike for anybody who wanted to try out snowshoeing. Even though my parents owned snowshoes, I had never actually been snowshoeing. It would be fun to try, but Max was going to lead the hike and I wasn't sure that I wanted to add any emotional awkwardness to the physical challenge.

"I wasn't planning on it, why?" I asked.

"Because I want to snowshoe and I need a ride there," Lennie said with a scowl. "My car has started acting up and it's your job to make sure your guests are happy. So the way to make me happy is to drive me to go snowshoe tomorrow."

I weighed that back and forth in my mind. Max was still really mad at me and I wasn't sure if I wanted to go on the snowshoe hike with him. But it might be a good way to get the murder off of my mind. I just couldn't figure out how to help Charlie and I needed a mental break from it. I finally settled on the fact that it might be a good idea to go hike, even if I had to steer clear of Max.

"Sure, I can do that," I said. I was pretty sure Max would stop being mad at me at some point but no matter what, we both lived in Shady Lake and avoiding him wasn't going to work forever. "The hike is supposed to start at 9, so meet me down here at 8:40 or so. I don't want to be late."

Lennie gave me a wave that acknowledged that he had heard what I said, and then turned and headed upstairs to his room. Living in a B&B was interesting because I was always being asked to do different things. My previous marketing job always seemed to be mostly the same thing day in and day out. Here, no day was the same or even similar to another. I could now add "chauffeur" to my resume, I guess.

•Chapter Twenty-Nine•

I had almost forgotten about my promise to myself to message Mandy but once I was relieved of desk duty and headed up to my bedroom, one look at the framed picture of us on my wall reminded me. Max's words played in my head about how Mandy only did so much for me because I couldn't handle it myself. The thought popped into my head that I may be doing this more because I felt guilty and not to help Mandy. I tried to shake that thought away and I typed out a message.

Manders, Want to come over and order a pizza with me? I feel like I haven't seen you in a while.

I know the pizza was pushing it a bit because Mandy was someone who liked to eat healthy, but I felt that part of my job as her best friend was to push her to let her hair down occasionally and spend a Friday night devouring pizza and watching bad movies.

I'll be right over.

I could tell that Mandy was still feeling a little hurt because she was usually a bit more long winded than that in her texts. I figured I could make up for it with some girl time.

Twenty minutes later, there was a knock on the door to the private section of the B&B and Mandy popped through the door with a hot and fresh Mike's pizza in her hand.

"Surprise," she said with a wide smile on her face. I certainly was surprised because normally she just went along with my unhealthy eating instead of being the one to encourage it.

I made it across the room in two big strides to take the pizza box off her hands. I cracked the top and admired the delicious, gooey pizza inside. Mike's made the best pizza in town because instead of shredded cheese, they layered sliced cheese on top. They had been making pizza this way at Mike's for decades and were considered a Shady Lake staple.

Besides the generous helping of sliced cheese on the top, the pizza also had pepperoni and sausage. Mandy knew the way to my heart. Between pizza and donuts, apparently the number one way to win me over is unhealthy food.

Once we were settled on the couch in front of the television with our pizza on some paper plates and a glass of wine each, I dug right in. The greasy smell was so delicious that I just couldn't wait.

"Tessa, I'm sorry for whatever I did," Mandy said. Her voice quavered.

I looked up from my plate with a mouthful of stringy cheese and saw that Mandy hadn't even touched her slice yet. A few tears were forming in her eyes and she blinked a few times, trying not to let me see. I tried to quickly swallow the wad of cheese in my mouth, but of course the fact that I was trying to hurry meant it took twice as long to actually swallow down.

"Why are you sorry?" I said when my mouth was finally clear. "I'm not mad at you. Where did you get that idea?"

"I just felt like you had been avoiding me," Mandy said. It felt like her words were punching me in the gut. Maybe Max was right. Maybe I was immature. "You didn't even text me after Chelsea ran that awful picture of you on the front page. I thought maybe I had asked too much of you when I asked you to help Trevor out."

I felt like the worst friend alive. I had let the fact that I was busy be my excuse for not talking to Mandy hardly at all this week. But Mandy was always busy. She ran the Donut Hut practically by herself and she still managed to stay up to date with me even when I was living in the Twin Cities.

"Why didn't you text me then?" I asked. "It isn't a great excuse, but I was just plain busy."

I could feel myself blushing a little bit because my excuse was super lame. Max's words kept ringing in the back of my mind. The pizza suddenly didn't look as appetizing as it had before I realized I was actually a bad friend. I set my plate down on the table and looked at Mandy again.

Winter Festival Murder

"I don't know," Mandy said. "You're right, I should have just text you. But I am glad you asked me to come over tonight because I do have some good news. Trevor is going back to college!"

I tried my hardest to act surprised, I really did. But I have never been good at that. I could instantly feel that I was really overselling my level of surprise. The loud squeal may have pushed it over the edge just a tad.

"You knew?" Mandy said. "How in the world did you know about that?"

"Trevor told me," I said. "And honestly, I'm pretty impressed with that. I know I'm really hard on Trevor, but it feels like he is finally starting to mature a little bit."

Mandy was beaming. Her pride for Trevor and his incredibly slow growth to maturity was shining off of her face and into every corner of the living room. For once, I was happy for her and Trevor instead of trying to a negative side of it.

"So now that I told you my good news, why don't you tell me about your investigation," Mandy said. Her eyes were still sparkling with pride for Trevor and I decided to tell her the good news first.

"I think I can pretty much rule out Trevor," I said. "It just doesn't make sense for him to be the killer. But on the other hand, I'm not sure Charlie is the killer. That leaves Lennie and Donna and neither of them make sense either."

"Hold on, back up and explain a little bit more please," Mandy said. "Remember, you haven't told me anything about it all week.

As I thought about where to begin, I grabbed another slice of pizza and put one on Mandy's plate too. She gave a little sigh, but started to grudgingly eat it.

"I guess my biggest thing is that no one has a real motive," I said. "Well, they do but none of the motives make that much sense. I just can't believe that someone killed Gerald so that he wouldn't find the medallion and win 500 dollars."

"That does seem like a pretty thin motive, even though Charlie and Lennie both made very public threats against Gerald," Mandy pointed out. She kept taking tiny nibbles of her pizza, just enough to get a taste.

"They did, but I have a feeling there is something else there that I either don't see or that I don't know," I said. "I feel like I may be stumped on this one."

We both finished our slices in silence. Call me a weirdo, but the crust is actually my favorite part of a slice of pizza. Pizza is great, but that carb-filled part at the end when you leave just enough cheese and sauce to flavor it a bit? Heaven in my mouth. I savored the crust until Mandy broke the silence.

Winter Festival Murder

"So what are you going to do now?" Mandy asked.

"I'm not sure," I said with a shrug. "I may just have to admit that maybe the police know what they are doing. I think for now I will just leave it be and watch some cheesy movies with you. Tomorrow I am going on the snowshoe hike and I'm also hoping to make Max be a little bit happier with me."

"Why is Max mad at you?"

I hadn't told Mandy about that either. As I ate a third slice and Mandy picked the sausage off of a third piece, I filled her in on the fight we had about the investigation ending with him saying I was immature. When I finished my story, Mandy put her plate on the table.

"It sounds like this investigation has really thrown you for a loop," she said as she shut the lid of the pizza box. This was her friendly way of telling me there is no way I need more than three slices of pizza and I was glad because at least if the box was closed, it was harder to see and smell that delicious pizza.

"Usually I'm pretty good at connecting clues and figuring out mysteries," I said with a sigh. "But this time is different. And the most annoying part is that I'll probably never know. The police have arrested Charlie and they have clues that they think fit, so that's the end of it."

It really was most disappointing and I was

sure Charlie felt the same way. I tried not to think too much about it because it made me too sad when I did.

Mandy took the box of pizza downstairs when she left to put it in the fridge where most likely Tank would eat the rest cold the next time he went looking for a snack. That was better for me because when the pizza is out of sight, it is definitely also out of mind.

Now if I could do the same for this mystery, I would be extra grateful because I needed some way to put it out of my mind.

•Chapter Thirty•

The nice thing about the fact that Mandy is a baker by trade is that our movie nights together ended really early. The donuts would not bake themselves early the next morning, so we were always done watching movies by 10 pm. Mandy always left with gentle encouragement that I should also go to bed. This time, I actually took her up on it.

I had an alarm set for 8 the next morning so that I would be up and ready for the snowshoe hike in time, but I actually woke up naturally and was happy to see that it was 7 in the morning. I stayed in bed for a few minutes before I decided to get up and help with breakfast downstairs. My parents would be up and serving breakfast in the dining room and I know they could always use another set of hands.

As soon as I was dressed and opened the door to the B&B, the delicious smells of breakfast hit me. It smelled like bacon and french toast this morning. One of the things I loved about the breakfast part of our bed and breakfast was that our breakfast wasn't uppity or difficult. It was always just a delicious, down home breakfast.

I found my father frying up bacon in the kitchen while my mother was making the french toast. I grabbed a coffee pot and went out to give

Winter Festival Murder

refills. We usually went through quite a few pots of coffee because our main crowd were senior citizens who were originally from Shady Lake, but now lived somewhere warm. They would come back to visit their grandchildren and our B&B was just a step above the motel in town that we also owned.

It seemed like the amount of coffee consumed by every adult in Minnesota went up with each passing year. I'm pretty sure once my parents hit middle age, the coffee pot in our house was only off when we were sleeping. Otherwise once it was empty, they just started it up again. I already seemed to drink coffee almost constantly, so I shuddered to think about drinking even more.

The table had six older couples having breakfast. Lennie was not present and one of the couples had gone out to meet their granddaughter for breakfast at the Breakfast Spot, so there were a few empty chairs. As I circled the table topping off everyone's coffee, I was congratulated on the snow sculpture competition three times. Living in a small town, I've learned that when something big happens, you just expect to have people comment on it constantly for at least a few weeks. That goes double or even triple if it is something that ends up on the front page of the Shady Lake Tribune like the terrible picture of me did.

"Is breakfast almost ready to go out?" I asked

as I brought the carafe of coffee back in to fill up. I poured some in my own coffee mug first and then filled up the carafe.

"Just let me fry up this last bit of bacon," my dad said. I grabbed a piece of bacon from the plate on the counter next to him and gobbled it up.

"You can take the french toast out while I get the toppings ready," my mother said.

I grabbed the two plates that were piled high with french toast slices and when I came back to the kitchen, I found my mother had bowls of fruit, pitchers of syrup, a dish of butter, and a little bowl of powdered sugar ready and waiting. Together we carried them all out to the table in a couple of trips and spread them up and down the middle.

The folks at breakfast were chattering away while they happily piled their plates high with breakfast. I was thanked profusely no less than four times, which was always pleasant. I couldn't imagine working in a bed and breakfast in another state because while we definitely got some grumpy characters, most of our guests were Minnesota Nice.

"You go get ready for that snowshoe hike," my mother said when we got back to the kitchen. "Don't be out too long. There is a nasty winter storm on the way."

My father topped up my coffee mug once more and I brought that with as I scurried off to the entryway. In Minnesota we believe that there isn't bad weather, just bad clothing. I grabbed my outerwear and drug it back into the living room because the entryway was just too drafty to get dressed in.

I glanced at the clock and saw that I had just enough time to layer up before Lennie was supposed to meet me. When they named the festival the Below Zero Festival, someone listened and made sure to match the weather to the name. I had already put on a pair of long underwear underneath my jeans and I threw on the sweater and sweatshirt on top of the long sleeve top I had put on.

A pair of snow pants was up next along with a fleece jacket, scarf, and warm winter jacket. I also had a stocking cap, my winter boots, and some mittens along with a pack of hand warmers to stuff inside, but I waited to put those on because I didn't want to overheat while waiting for Lennie to come down. A glance at the clock told me that if he was on time, he would be down in about two minutes to meet me. Perfect timing on my part.

I sat down in one of the armchairs by the front door and looked outside. Obviously it was cold, but at least it didn't look windy. Growing up in Minnesota had shown me that it wasn't the cold that made things miserable but the wind certainly did. Freezing cold wind could cut through outerwear like it was nothing, even if you layered up. But this morning looked still with the trees standing straight up.

One phenomenon Minnesotans use to see how cold it is without looking at a thermometer is by looking at the sun for sun dogs. When it is very cold, there will be two bright spots, one on either side of the sun, with what appears to be an arc going between them. Technically, I've learned that it doesn't have to be super cold for them to appear, but they are much more common on freezing cold days like today. Today, there were two very prominent spots of light out there. I took that as a pretty good sign that it was a cold one out there.

I felt myself starting to sweat and I looked at the clock again. I'd told Lennie to meet me five minutes ago and he was nowhere in sight. My thoughts turned towards Max again. He hadn't talked to me since that night he got mad at me and I realized that I hadn't messaged him either. I wasn't sure what to say because Max was partially right; I did sometimes use him to get more information about cases the police were investigating. He also seemed to be right about me being immature, but that would take some time to work on.

But I wasn't using him in a bad way. What I meant was that it wasn't the only reason I went out with Max. It was more of an added bonus to going out with a police officer. I could see his point, though. Maybe I was getting too into these mysteries and forgetting about the fact that they involved real people. I needed to try to scale things back a bit.

Now I was sweltering in all of this outerwear besides feeling a bit embarrassed by how I had treated Max. I stripped off my jackets and scarf, trying to save myself from melting. If I got too comfortable in my outdoor gear inside, I'd be freezing cold during our snowshoe hike. That is, if we were going on the hike. Lennie was still nowhere in sight and the hike was going to leave in about five minutes.

I stood up from the armchair, resigned to the fact that the hike was just not going to happen today. That was alright though. I needed to figure out how to apologize to Max. I started to unbutton my snow pants.

"Where's your jacket? We need to go. We are going to be late."

I turned and saw Lennie coming down the stairs, fully dressed in his outdoor gear. He looked fully annoyed to find me undressing which was rich coming from someone who was coming down 15 minutes late.

"We're mostly going to be late because you are running late," I said as I wound my scarf back around my neck. "How are we going to know where to hike if they've left without us?"

"I don't think it's that kind of hike," Lennie said as I put my jackets on. "I think you can go with the big group if you want. But I also think they have the trail marked for anyone who wants to hike it without the group."

I rolled my eyes as I jammed my hat on my head. I grabbed my mittens and the keys to the station wagon. My phone was already in one of my inner pockets. I wasn't sure I could even find it in all of my layers, but I wouldn't need it.

"Let's go," I said. I whipped open the front door and plowed my way out into the cold with Lennie hot on my heels.

•Chapter Thirty-One•

If I had thought ahead, I would have gone out and started the station wagon while I was waiting for Lennie to come downstairs. I guess I was kind of hoping it meant I wouldn't have to go face Max at the snowshoe hike. Instead, we were now stuck sitting in a freezing cold car. I made a note to ask for an automatic car starter to be put in for either my birthday or next Christmas, not that it would help us now.

The cloudy puffs of air that came out of our mouths hung in the air in front of our faces. At least the windshield didn't need to be scraped this morning. I assumed that someone had already done it for me and I felt a sudden rush of thankfulness for my family.

Lennie and I sat in silence for a few minutes while we waited for the car to warm up a little bit before heading out. I glanced at the clock and saw that we were already five minutes past the meeting time for the hike. Lennie better be right about them marking out the trail for those of us that can't manage to be on time. At least I wouldn't have to worry about being too close to Max.

Finally, I felt like I had let my poor, old car warm up enough to not immediately die in the cold weather, so we headed towards the snowshoe hike. The hike was taking place in a big park that was within the town boundaries, but was so large that it was useful for things like this snowshoe hike. It was situated next to the old country club that had closed down a few years ago and now the old golf holes had kind of been tacked onto the side of the park almost as an unofficial extra green space.

As I drove around the lake towards the park, I could see Lennie shifting around in his seat next to me. It was like he couldn't stop moving and I wondered what was wrong with him. But like always with Lennie, I didn't know whether I should say something or not. I always seemed to pick the wrong one.

Finally, out of sheer curiosity, I decided to say something.

"What's wrong?" I asked as I kept my eyes on the road. I figured that would help the conversation a little bit. "Why are you moving around so much?"

"I just can't get comfortable," Lennie growled.

"Why do you have to be comfortable?" I asked. "It isn't like we are driving that far."

"Just shut it and drive," Lennie said. "We're already late."

I grumbled to myself. We were late because of him, but I decided not to remind him of that. I was having a grouchy enough day and poking the bear was not going to make that any better.

The streets were a little icy and as I tried to turn into the parking lot of the park, I slid sideways a bit up and over the curb as I turned the steering wheel into the same direction as the sliding back end of the station wagon.

"Ope, sorry 'bout that," I said. It didn't matter how many sand bags you put in the back of this old station wagon, it was still going to slide around on the winter roads. I was used to it by now. I had to get used to it if I ever wanted to go anywhere during the winter.

Lennie just scowled harder, which I didn't think was possible until I watched his face shrivel up more.

I pulled the station wagon into a spot and put it in park. The parking lot was full of cars, but strangely there didn't seem to be anyone there. In front of the car was a large building that was rented out for parties and other events. I assumed we would need to go inside there to check in before we started the hike. But before I could shut the car off, Lennie stopped me.

"Hold on," he said. "I wanted to ask you something. It's about Gerald's, umm, death."

"You mean the murder?" I asked. Lennie's eyes darted around the car and I felt like maybe I shouldn't have brought up the word murder if he was going to act so weird. Maybe he just felt guilty about having threatened Gerald. Or maybe, and this was more likely in my mind, he was more upset about the medallion hunt being cut short and figured that maybe if Gerald's death was solved fast enough, the hunt would be back on. That would explain why he extended his reservation at the B&B. "What did you want to know?"

"Well, did you ever solve it?" he asked like it was something I had just figured out in my spare time one day and had told nobody about.

"I wouldn't say I solved it, but I have a strong feeling that I know who did it," I said, narrowing my eyes at him. If he was going to be a jerk to me, I was going to make it seem like I knew exactly who had done it. Maybe that would show him and he'd treat me a little better. I pushed back the thought that this may be the immaturity that Max was talking about in action.

"You know who did it," Lennie said slowly and evenly.

"Sure I do," I said. "In fact, I was planning on going to the police later today to tell them what I knew."

The air was still inside the car and I felt like time had slowed down. There didn't seem to be anyone else here. Were we wrong about where the snowshoe hike started? How come no one was here?

Winter Festival Murder

"I wouldn't do that if I were you," Lennie said. "It might be dangerous for you."

Lennie was shifting around in his seat again. This time, I looked over and one of the large cargo pockets on the outside of his coat fell open and I could see two things inside: a gold coin and a handgun.

"Is that the medallion from the medallion hunt?" I asked slowly. Suddenly the car felt very warm and very small. If time was slow before, it felt like it had stopped now.

"Yes it is Tessa," Lennie said. He was staring at me and his eyes were wild. "Sorry to spoil your surprise, but I was the one who found the medallion. And I can't let you turn me in."

My mind was racing a million miles a minute and I just couldn't seem to put any sort of plan into place for myself. Should I try to jump out of the car? Should I try to drive somewhere? Before I could make a decision, Lennie made the decision for me.

"Here is what we are going to do," Lennie said. He casually put his hand on the gun, almost as a warning to me. "We are going to get out of the car and join the snowshoe hike."

I started to protest, but Lennie stopped me by tightening his hand on his gun.

"Ah ah ah, no arguing," he said, waving the pointer finger on his other hand in my face. "I have a plan and you are going to do as I say. I'm a pretty good shot, so don't try anything."

He opened his door and stepped out, motioning me to hurry up. I shut the car off and got out, grabbing my snowshoes out of the back of the car for us. Lennie jerked his head towards the park building in front of us and I started that way.

I had a realization that Max was the one leading the snowshoe hike. If I could find him, I could get his help. Maybe they hadn't left yet. Maybe they were all inside preparing for the hike. Now I just needed to stay calm and figure out where Max and the rest of the hike were. No matter how upset Max might still be, he would help me.

Winter Festival Murder

•Chapter Thirty-Two•

I pushed open the double doors of the park building. The main room was decorated in a rustic cabin style and was large enough to handle gatherings like graduation parties, birthday parties, or even a small wedding reception. On one side, there was a kitchenette with a large island counter where currently a large coffee urn and a picked-over tray of cookies was set up. On the other side was a wall of windows except for a large fireplace with a roaring fire that was centered in the middle. Dotted all through the rest of the room were large, round tables.

I was hoping I would see people bustling around getting ready for the hike. I was especially hoping to see Max getting ready. It didn't matter that he was mad at me, I knew that if he was inside, I would be able to signal to him that something was wrong and that I needed help.

Instead, the building was empty except for Donna, who was cleaning up some paper cups that were sitting on table around the room and little Bobby, who was running around with a toy car in his hand, lost in his own world of childhood.

A sudden wave of guilt washed over me. Why had I thought it was a good idea to lead a killer with a gun into a place with innocent people, including children? Of all the times that I had wished that I'd stopped to think, this seemed like it was the worst one of all.

I took a deep breath. I needed to clear my head because the only one to blame here was Lennie. It wouldn't have been a good idea to go against what he was saying, so I didn't have much choice, did I? I made a quick decision to just try to plow forward with my plan to get Max's help.

"Hi Donna," I said. I tried to sound casual, but I ended up sounding like I was dementedly happy. "Where are all of the snowshoe hikers?"

"Oh you just missed them," she said with a smile, her hands full of paper cups. "But if you hurry and get your snowshoes on, you might be able to catch up or at least follow along from a distance. Hold on, let me see."

Donna walked over to the wall of windows and glanced out. Bobby was playing some sort of game with himself and as I watched him happily playing, my mind flashed back to the gun in Lennie's pocket. I needed to get Lennie out of here and away from Bobby.

"Oh yeah, see there they are," Donna said, pointing outside. I joined her next to the window.

She was right. I could just see the group of snowshoers across part of the field that was next to the park building. If we could get our snowshoes on fast enough, maybe we could catch them. The only problem would be that I'd never actually been snowshoeing before. Oh, and the gun was also a problem, I suppose.

"Let's go Lennie," I said, grabbing my snowshoes and heading out the door. I wanted to get Lennie out of there as fast as I possibly could. Thankfully, Lennie followed me out into the cold. The wind was starting to pick up. I just hoped that the storm would hold off for just a little while.

Snow had started to fall and I took a seat on a park bench outside to figure out how to get the snowshoes on. My dad showed me how to do put them on correctly and I hoped that I would be able to get them on fast enough to get out of here and catch up with Max.

I jammed my boots down onto the snowshoes and tightened the straps around them as fast as I could, feeling grateful that it was easier than I remembered. Lennie plopped down next to me on the bench and set his snowshoes down on the snow in front of him. He slowly started to strap his feet onto them. I couldn't tell if he was doing it to annoy me or because he just didn't know what he was doing.

Finally I dropped to my knees on the snow and strapped them to his feet myself. If we didn't get out of here soon, we would never catch up with the group. But I couldn't just leave Lennie behind. I have no idea if he is a good shot or not, but I wasn't going to risk it now that I had snowshoes strapped to my feet.

The last of the hiking group was just rounding a corner behind a row of pine trees. We needed to get a move on or we would never catch them. If I could at least get closer to them, I figured I could try to get Max's attention.

"Come on, let's get a move on," I said.

•Chapter Thirty-Three•

I turned and promptly fell on my face into a large drift of snow. My legs tangled together and while trying to untangle them, I managed to kick myself in the shins a few times. I could feel bruises instantly start to bloom on both legs. Okay, so snowshoeing may be a bit harder than I thought.

But I couldn't give up hope. If I didn't at least try to catch up with Max, I would be stuck with a killer here at the park building and I couldn't do that to Donna and Bobby. So I did the only thing I could: I awkwardly picked myself up and out of the snow.

Lennie was still sitting on the bench snickering at both my fall and my awkward attempts to get up. I would have gotten angry if he hadn't been carrying a gun, but instead I just scowled to myself as I brushed the snow off of my front.

"Let's go," I growled again. Lennie just snickered again, but at least he stood up from the bench this time.

I started out again, this time looking down at my feet to make sure I wasn't stepping on my own snowshoes. It was odd, but after a few steps I started to get the hang of it. If I kept part of my mind on the snowshoes, I just might be able to catch up with those hikers.

Winter Festival Murder

Behind me, Lennie was taking his sweet time. I couldn't help but be a little annoyed, both at Lennie for threatening me and at myself for stupidly walking myself into this whole trap.

"Come on," I said. "You're going too slow."

"Oh I'm sorry," he said sarcastically. "I forgot you wanted to come to catch up with your cop boyfriend. Let me just speed up so that you can tell him that I'm the killer and I'm carrying a gun."

Darn, he had picked up on that right away. I was hoping he'd be so focused on me that he wouldn't figure out what I was trying to do. But the one plan I'd thought up was now totally blown. I needed to just keep moving forward while I tried to figure something else out.

Lennie burst out laughing again behind me. It was a loud, gut laugh that immediately got on my nerves. I hadn't even fallen down, what did he possibly have to laugh about? I tried to wait it out, but he just kept going until I whirled around.

"What?" I shouted. "What is so funny to you?"

"Oh, I was just thinking again about how I foiled your little plot," Lennie said. "You totally thought I was going to let us catch up with that group where you could tell that cop all about me. It is just hilarious. You know, you aren't as smart as you try to be."

I started to boil with anger inside. It was one

thing when I thought I wasn't smart. It was quite another when someone else tried to tell me that. Especially because it was Lennie's own stupidity that had gotten him here in the first place.

Instead of saying something that might get me shot, I turned and plowed forward. The snow and wind seemed like it was starting to pick up but besides having a cold face, the rest of me was quite warm. Score one for learning to layer up.

The bank of trees that the hiking group had turned behind was coming up and I couldn't wait to round that corner and figure out a way to get Max's attention. The line of trees had been planted too close together originally and now they had gotten so big that they were all intertwined in a row. I couldn't see through the branches to see how fast or slow the rest of the group was going. I just needed to pick up speed and get around that corner.

I stumbled again, getting so excited that I stepped on my own snowshoe. My body pitched forward and my arms flailed wildly. I managed to keep my balance but decided I needed to just focus on staying up right and making it around the corner.

Lennie laughed again from behind me and I couldn't ignore it this time. His laugh wasn't a spontaneous one that you just can't quite stifle. It was loud and braying, meant to annoy.

"What exactly is so funny?" I asked. "I've never

been on snowshoes before today."

"This is the first time?" Lennie said, howling with laughter. "Oh that is rich. Out of all the times to try out snowshoeing, you picked to do it with a man with a gun. Hilarious!"

"I take it you've been snowshoeing before?" I asked.

"I've snowshoed my entire life," Lennie said, puffing up his chest. "I grew up way out in the country and my family loved to snowshoe. Sometimes if a big enough storm came, it was the only way to get anywhere. We would snowshoe into town to get more supplies. Some of us didn't grow up soft, like you."

Leave it to Lennie to be Mr. Pioneer with his snowshoes. I ignored him, stomping on in the snow. I couldn't let him get my goat because he was definitely the one with the upper hand right now.

The wind was picking up and every time it hit me, it was an ice cold blast to the face. I wish I would have looked closer at the weather forecast before we came out. The sky was dark gray and I wondered if the storm was coming sooner than the meteorologist had originally said. But there was definitely a different kind of storm brewing around that line of trees. I just needed to plow on and get there.

•Chapter Thirty-Four•

I was almost around the corner, past the trees. My hope bubbled up. I was almost to safety. If I could just get around there and get Max's help, this would be all over with. Lennie was about five snowshoe steps behind me. No matter how fast I was going, Lennie would pick up the pace and stay right with me. I guess when you grow up snowshoeing, it is much easier to keep a steady pace.

Finally, I was at the big pine tree that stood at the end of the line of trees. It was over sized, the kind of pine tree that grew wild without anyone ever trying to trim the branches or make it bend to their will. The branches stretched out, all tangled together and trying to take up as much space as possible.

I made it around the tree and the giant bubble of hope that had been in my stomach burst. There were actually two long lines of trees that formed a sort of private avenue and there was no one in sight. Well, I could faintly see two or three bright jackets that were just rounding the corner at the end of the long line of trees and the snow showed a lot of snowshoe tracks from when the group had tramped through, but everyone was gone.

"Let's go," Lennie said, clapping his hand onto my shoulder as he passed me for the first time during the hike.

I briefly thought about turning to run back to the safety of the park building, but I wasn't able to run with snowshoes on my feet and even if I could get them off, I'd just be leading a man with a gun back towards Donna and Bobby. I would just have to face him here.

I followed Lennie into the avenue of trees, trying to look through the other side to see where the group had gone. Of course, the second row of trees were just as overgrown as the first so I couldn't see anything through them. Maybe they were just swinging around the second row of trees and heading back to the park building. It was hard to see anything through the branches, but there were no signs of life through there. No colorful jackets or sounds of happiness. I was on my own with the killer.

"Come on over here," Lennie said. I could tell he is teasing me.

He was standing in the middle of the avenue of trees and I knew I didn't have much of a choice, so I walked a little ways towards him before I stopped. I had to ask him some more questions just so I could understand what exactly was going on.

"I know you're going to try and shoot me, but before you do, you have to answer a few questions," I said.

"I don't have to do anything," Lennie said.

Winter Festival Murder

He took his mittens off and pulled the gun out of his pocket. I couldn't help but think about how cold his fingers were going to get because the temperature was dropping even more. I pulled myself back a bit before actually feeling bad for his cold fingers and I snapped back into the reality that he was currently pointing a gun at me.

"First of all, you knew the hike would be gone when we got here, didn't you?" I asked.

"I came down to scope out the hike area yesterday," Lennie's face curled up into an evil grin. "Once I knew you figured out that it was me, I came up with this plan. I knew that if I could stall us just enough, the hike would leave and we would be able to have this nice spot all to ourselves."

I had to give him some credit. He had really thought through this plan. I wondered if he had put as much care and effort into murdering Gerald. I may as well just ask. I didn't want to die curious.

"I have to say that I'm impressed with your planning," I said. "I bet you put a lot of thought into killing Gerald as well."

Lennie's face fell. The evil grin that had been planted there slid down into an expression that I couldn't read and that I was definitely not expecting. If he hadn't been brandishing a gun, I would have felt bad for him once again.

"I hadn't planned on killing Gerald," Lennie

said. I could barely hear him over the whipping wind and while I didn't want to get any closer to him, I did grudgingly take a few more steps towards him so that I could hear him better.

"Sure you did," I said. "I've seen the crime scene. I know that whoever killed Gerald waited in that bank of trees behind the park bench until he came to find the medallion. Apparently it wasn't good enough to just find the medallion, you had to get Gerald too."

Lennie was violently shaking his head back and forth and I could see a few tears on his cheeks. I had to imagine it was hard to be confronted with the details of a crime you had committed.

"So you waited until Gerald came to get the medallion and you jumped out and killed him," I said. "He did not deserve to die."

I was really on a roll now and I couldn't stop myself. I don't care how much of a jerk Gerald was or that he cheated at a stupid medallion hunt. No one deserved to be murdered in such cold blood.

"Sure, he cheated, but that doesn't mean he should be killed for it," I said. "Shame on you."

The gun wobbled around wildly as Lennie's hand started to shake. Tears were rolling down his face. I had a hard time believing that this man who couldn't hold it together had already murdered one other person.

Winter Festival Murder

"Well come on," I said. I was starting to get angry now. Why couldn't he keep it together? "Tell me all about how Gerald deserved to die and how you were just ridding the world of a cheater. That's what you're going to say, right?"

Lennie let out a big sob and when I looked at him, he had on one of the ugliest crying faces I've ever seen. It almost made me angry. Isn't this just all old hat for him now? I should have keep my mouth shut, but I just couldn't help myself.

"What's wrong?" I yelled. The wind was whipping now and I had to yell for him to hear me even though we were only a few steps away from each other. "Pull it together. You're going to kill me soon, right? You planned it all out just like you planned out the fact that you were going to kill Gerald too."

"But I didn't!" Lennie yelled. He dropped the gun to to his side. "I didn't plan it. Killing Gerald was an accident."

I stepped back like he had struck me. What did he mean it was an accident? How was a murder an accident? But looking at his face, he didn't look like he was lying or trying to lead me astray. He truly believed it was an accident.

•Chapter Thirty-Five•

There we stood in the middle of the avenue of trees. The wind whipped snowflakes all around us. The tiny snowflakes felt like little ice balls when they hit me in the face. I stared at Lennie and he was staring right back at me. It felt like I had lost all track of time. How long had we been in these trees?

The sky was fully gray now and the storm had definitely blown in. Snow was falling hard and the wind was blowing it everywhere so that it was starting to be whiteout conditions out here. The storm was here and instead of being warm and cozy in the B&B, I was outside attempting to snowshoe away from a killer. All hopes I had of being rescued were gone now. The only person who could save me now was me.

"What do you mean it was an accident?" I shouted over the roar of the wind. "How do you accidentally kill someone?"

"Maybe not accidentally, but it was self-defense," Lennie said.

I decided to take a chance and take a few more steps closer so that I could actually hear what he was saying.

"What do you mean Lennie."

I was so close to him now that the clouds of

breath that came out of his mouth flowed directly into my face. Any other time, this would have been too close for comfort. But I knew that I couldn't miss what he was about to tell me. This entire time with Lennie had been leading up to this moment.

"I mean that I didn't take the medallion from Gerald," Lennie said, pulling the coin out of his pocket and holding it up. "I found the medallion. I won this year, but no one will ever know that."

Lennie started to ugly cry again. Tears started to run down his face and his nose was running. It was cold enough out that I was sure my nose was probably boogery too, but crying had turned his nose on like a faucet.

"I've worked all of these years to finally win," he said, dragging the mitten clad hand holding the medallion beneath his nose to wipe away the snot. "I thought this year was finally my year because Hilda's poetic clues would be gone and no one would be able to replace them. And I was right. Props to Max for making the clues rhyme, but they were pretty obvious."

I had to agree with them. Max had made a valiant effort, but compared to Hilda's treasure hunt, these clues had seemed much more obvious. It was understandable that even if Gerald hadn't been cheating, someone would have thought they had a better chance this year.

Winter Festival Murder

"I figured out that the medallion must be at Evergreen Park, so I drove over and parked in the parking lot to scout it out a little bit," Lennie said. "I didn't want to give away that I was looking for the medallion, so I just looked around from the car. Really, those trees and that bench were the only places the medallion would be hidden in that park. So I made a plan to come back right when it was getting dark so that I could look without giving it away."

"And do you think Gerald saw you?" I asked. I still couldn't believe that people would go so crazy over a medallion hunt, even one with a minimal cash prize.

"He must have seen me, because when I came back later that night, he was waiting for me," Lennie said.

His face was hurt, his eyebrows drawn together in confusion. Lennie was looking towards me, but he wasn't seeing me. He was reliving the night of Gerald's murder. The wind was blowing even more than before, but he didn't seem to notice.

"I parked and grabbed a flashlight so that I could see what I was doing," Lennie continued on with his story. "I actually fell a few times as I was trying to get down that slippery hill. Stupid, why didn't I just use the sidewalk on the side? But I finally got down there and I started looking at the bench."

As he spoke, emotions flashed across his face.

Winter Festival Murder

The tears that had slowed down at one point started to fall more rapidly again. As the story ramped up, so did his emotions. For a moment, I forgot about the gun and I just felt sorry for him.

"I had just spotted the glint of gold when all of a sudden, Gerald burst out of the trees," Lennie shouted. "He came charging at me, yelling and screaming at me that I couldn't be the one to find the medallion. But he was too late, I already had it in my hands."

Lennie looked down at the medallion in his hand. He stared at it for a moment, seeming to forget about the gun he was still holding in his other hand. At least, I was hoping he had forgot about it.

"I told Gerald that his cheating days were over and I'd found it fair and square," Lennie said. "That's when he pulled out the gun. He pointed it at me and told me to give him the medallion or he would shoot me."

The hand holding the gun lifted back up to point at me. I couldn't tell if Lennie was just acting out the story, or meaning to point it at me. I took a deep breath to try and calm myself, which was not easy to do with a gun pointed directly at me.

"I refused," Lennie continued. "I didn't think he would actually shoot me over the medallion. And he didn't want to because instead of just shooting me, he lunged at me and tried to wrestle me down into the snow. I wasn't going to let him get the upper hand and I certainly wasn't going to let him shoot me. So as he came towards me, I grabbed for the gun."

Lennie's hand started to shake and the gun was waving all over the place, but always pointed in my general direction. I tried to keep my eye both on it and on Lennie's face. I was trying to take in all of the details I could just in case I was able to get out of this alive.

"Gerald was so focused on the medallion, he just kept trying to grab it from me," Lennie said. His voice dropped down even quieter and I leaned in a little closer, trying to be able to hear him without getting too close to him. "I was able to grab the gun and before Gerald could do anything, I turned it on him and I shot him."

Somehow the roar of the wind seemed to be drowned out by Lennie's silence. This story had flipped everything I thought I had known about the murder. It felt like forever that we stood and stared at each other while I ran over the story Lennie had told me in my head.

"Lennie, why didn't you call the police?" I finally said. "If it was self-defense like you say it was, why didn't you just call and tell them that."

Lennie snorted and let out a guffaw. I hoped I hadn't made him angry because I really didn't want to die out here in this snow storm. As he laughed to himself, I took a quick glance around, but all I could see was the blinding white of blowing snow and the tree branches swaying around me.

"Do you really think they would have believed it was self-defense?" Lennie asked. "After I publicly threatened Gerald, I don't think they would have believed me for an instant."

"So this was what you thought would work better?" I shouted. I was starting to get angry. I had been dragged into all of this because a grown man couldn't take responsibility of his actions. I tried to ignore the fact that immaturity was also my downfall. "Has this turned out the way you were hoping? Is luring me here to try to kill me really a plan that will work out for you? I'm sure they'll figure out it was you because multiple people saw you and I together and knew I was taking you here to snowshoe. And once they figure out that you killed me, they are going to connect you to Gerald's murder too. You aren't going to get away with any of this."

By the end, I was practically screaming in Lennie's face, both because I was so angry and because the wind was loud and I wanted him to hear every word I was saying. He needed to know exactly what was going to happen.

Lennie shoved my shoulder, making me stumble back a few steps and sit down hard on my bottom. As I tried to stand up with the snowshoes on my feet, Lennie pointed the gun straight for me again. And now the fire inside of him had exploded into anger that was radiating out of his eyes.

    I just couldn't keep my mouth shut and now I was really in trouble.

•Chapter Thirty-Six•

I started to formulate a plan in my head, but I had no idea if it was going to work. In fact, it seemed like an entirely idiotic idea but it was the only thing I could think of. I decided it was now or never. Either way, I might get shot, but I'd rather get shot trying to get away.

Lennie was glaring at me, his teeth clenched into a grimace. With one hand, he was pointing the gun directly at me while the other was still holding his precious medallion. The only thing stopping me from running right now was the fact that I was wearing snowshoes. I needed to get them off of my feet as fast as possible.

Suddenly, I snapped my head to look just past Lennie, over one of his shoulders. I was hoping I could fool him into distraction. In my peripheral vision, I could see him pull his eyebrows together in confusion.

"What are you looking at?" he demanded while waving his gun around.

"Nothing," I said, looking back at the spot over his shoulder. I shifted so that one snowshoe was standing on top of the other one. I wiggled my one foot to loosen up the ties on my snow boots, glad I had not followed my dad's advice to tightly lace them up while snowshoeing.

"Tell me what's over there," he said.

"There is nothing over there," I said. I shifted my weight so that I was trying to loosen my other boot.

Lennie wouldn't take my word for it, so he slowly turned to look over his shoulder. As soon as he turned his head, I lunged forward and grabbed the medallion out of his hand before dancing back a few steps. I managed to get one foot out of the boot and as I stepped down into the snow with it, I was glad that at least I was wearing wool socks today.

"Give that back," he shouted. He started to plead with me. "Please give it to me. I won the medallion fair and square this year."

As he begged for me to give him his prize back, I stepped out of my other boot and into the snow. Lennie was so focused on the medallion that he hadn't noticed that I had abandoned the snowshoes. So far, so good. Now to continue on to the next part of the plan.

"You want it that bad?" I asked. I held the medallion up over my head. Lennie's eyes followed it like a dog looking at a tennis ball. I waved it back and forth a few times before I pulled my arm back. "Then go find it."

I launched the medallion as far as I could over Lennie's head and into the swirling snow. He turned and watched helplessly as it disappeared. I waited for a moment to see what he would do, hoping his devotion to finding the medallion would make him go after that instead of me.

Lennie stood sideways, looking back and forth a few times between me and where I had tossed the medallion. My stocking feet were rapidly getting cold and I just hoped they wouldn't freeze too fast.

"I won that medallion fair and square," he shouted.

For a moment, I thought he was going to lunge at me and attack me. I could see in his eyes that he wanted to. But instead he ran the other way, looking around frantically for the medallion. He glanced back at me once, but after that I knew I needed to take my chance.

I turned and started to run back the way we came, but I knew that if it somehow stopped blowing snow around, I would be as good as dead. It was almost like I was running down a hallway made of trees. He had a clear shot towards me and I needed to change that. I made a sharp right turn and ran straight through the line of trees.

The tree branches hit me in the face and I could feel the pine needles scratching my cheeks. The rest of me was covered in my winter clothes, but I could feel the branches catching and ripping my jacket and snow pants. I pushed on until I popped out the other side of the branches. As I ran, I realized my stocking hat had come off of my head, so I grabbed my hood and pulled it up over my head, cinching the drawstrings to keep my ears under cover and warm.

I couldn't see the park building through the blowing snow, but I knew that if I just kept running, I should run straight into it. While it made me a little nervous to be running blind, it did give me comfort that the blowing snow also offered me some cover.

My feet were starting to get so cold that I couldn't feel my toes anymore. If I had the strength to worry about that, I would have. But I needed to focus all I could on getting out of the snow and getting help. My father had suggested I layer my socks and thankfully, I had listened to him about that. But the cold and wet were seeping in and the only thing that was going to stop it was changing my socks.

From behind me, I heard a faint pop sound. Lennie must be shooting at me. I might be hearing things, but I chose to believe it was a gunshot. He must have just realized I had ran away.

A bit of panic started to set in, but thankfully a building started to materialize through the blowing snow just a few yards in front of me. I had done it; I had made it back to the building. I couldn't remember where the doors were, but as I came up to the windows, I could see the rest of the snowshoeing hike had come back to warm up inside.

Winter Festival Murder

I started to pound on the window as I heard another faint pop behind me. I looked, but I couldn't tell if Lennie was getting closer or if he was still back in the avenue of trees, shooting aimlessly towards where he thought I might be.

Turning back to the window, most of the hikers were focused on their hot chocolate and cookies, oblivious to my knocking. I pounded as hard as I could, hoping I could get someone's attention.

"Tessa!"

Max's voice was coming from somewhere to my right. I started to scramble that way until I could see his head popping out of a door.

"Tessa, what in the world is going on?" he said. "Come in before you freeze!"

He pulled me in the door where a small group of concerned townspeople had congregated. Donna was holding a tray of cookies which Ronald was happily helping himself to. Max looked down and noticed my stocking feet.

"What happened to your boots?" Max said. "Are you crazy going out without something on your feet? Sit down, we need to warm you up right now. Donna, get something with warm water for her feet. If we don't warm them up soon, she is going to have frostbite."

Donna scurried off to the kitchenette while Max took me by the arms and pushed me down into a chair. He started to peel the socks off of my feet so that he could inspect my toes and see if they were too far gone.

"I don't care about my feet right now," I said. "Lennie is trying to kill me."

Max looked up at me from where he was kneeling on the floor. I realized that he probably thought I had some sort of medical condition. I stumbled in out of a blizzard with no boots or hat and now I was claiming that a killer was after me. I needed to make him understand otherwise we would all be in danger.

"I don't have time to tell you the full story right now," I said. "But Lennie is out there. He killed Gerald and when he thought I figured him out, he lured me out there to kill him. I managed to run away, but he has a gun and he will be heading here any minute."

CLANG

The large metal bowl filled with warm water that Donna had been carrying over for me to put my feet in crashed to the floor. Donna's eyes were wide and wild and she started to frantically look around the room.

"What do you mean he's heading here?" she yelled. "Bobby! Bobby, where are you."

As Donna ran around the room, a quiet murmur spread from one side of the room to the other. Everyone was passing on what they had just heard me say. Soon enough, it had reached the other end of the large gathering space and almost as if it had been timed, everyone frantically started to grab their jackets and tumble out into the parking lot and the whipping wind.

"Here's what we are going to do," Max said as everyone else abandoned their snacks. "I'm going to get you some warm water for your feet. You are going to hide yourself over behind the counter of the kitchenette while I call for an ambulance and some backup."

I nodded. I hoped both of those would come soon because I had already escaped a killer once today and I wasn't sure I could do it again.

Winter Festival Murder

•Chapter Thirty-Seven•

Max picked me up and carried me over to the kitchenette area. He helped me take off my jacket and then he spread it on the ground. I scooted myself onto it so that I had at least a little bit of a cushion beneath me. He quickly filled the metal bowl with warm water again and helped me set my feet in it. It hurt and felt good at the same time and it reminded me why we always dress warm in the winter, even if we are tough Minnesotans.

"Okay, I put in a quick call for help while I was filling up the bowl," Max said. "They said they would send everyone out as soon as they could. I just wish we could see where Lennie was. It makes me nervous not knowing."

I nodded as I tried not to grimace about the pain in my feet. I noticed that Max had drawn his gun, just in case we were taken by surprise. I had a feeling we wouldn't be. I hadn't even been able to find the door and I assumed Lennie wouldn't be able to find it either. But I had also assumed he wasn't the killer and look where that got us.

"Max, I'm sorry that I used you to get more information," I said. I put my hand on his knee. "Sometimes I get so excited about solving these puzzles that I forget how it may feel for you."

"It's alright, Tessa," Max said. He glanced at me quickly, but went right back to scouting the area. The brief look I did get made me feel a little better.

"Besides, apparently you were right," Max said. "We had the wrong guy in custody and you knew it."

"We can call it even," I said. "Because even though I knew Charlie didn't do it, I hadn't really figured out it was Lennie until he practically told me."

Max chuckled and I couldn't help laughing along with him. What a ridiculous situation we were in, but I was glad I was in it with Max. There was no one else I'd rather hide from a killer in a blizzard from than him.

Suddenly, Max's phone buzzed. He picked it up and answered.

"Go," he said, listening to whoever was on the other end. "I'll let you in, hold on."

Max glanced at me and I nodded. He darted out from behind the counter and rushed towards the front door. When he got back, another young officer named Philip was following him. Philip was a few years younger than Max and I, with red hair that was gelled back out of his eyes. His blue eyes were big with worry and I wondered how much help he would actually be.

"So, there's a killer out there, huh?" Philip said. He was trying hard to be casual, but his voice shook. If I hadn't been stuck soaking my feet, I would have tried to comfort him myself.

"Listen to me, Philip," Max said. "I need you to sit here and make sure Tessa is safe. Do not leave her side, not even when the ambulance gets here. You will go with her in the ambulance and only when she is safely at the hospital will you leave her side."

Philip nodded. He kept one hand on the gun that was strapped to his side and I was glad he wasn't taking it out of the holster because I had a feeling he would not be a very straight shot right now. Max looked at his phone where I could see there was an incoming message.

"I'm going to let a few more officers in," Max said. He slid out from behind the counter and I was left with Philip.

"It's going to be okay," I told him. He looked at me, his eyes still wide with shock. I'm sure being a Shady Lake police officer means he doesn't chase killers or really any kind of criminals that often. In fact, I would put money on the fact that this was probably the first time for him.

Max returned with three more officers. I wasn't sure how many more officers were going to come, but I kind of hoped the ambulance wouldn't show up until after they found Lennie. I'd been through so much that I deserved to be able to see the resolution to all of this.

"Tessa, tell us a quick version of what

happened please," Max said. He had his police officer voice on now and my loving Max had transitioned to being all business right now.

I relayed the story of Lennie and I on the snowshoe hike. I told them how I had seen the medallion and how he made me go on the hike out to the rows of trees. I told them about Lennie's story and how he had killed Gerald in self-defense. Then, I told them about how I had escaped him and found my way here.

By the end of my story, the expressions on the faces of the officers had all caved in from serious police officer to wide-eyed audience member. While I enjoyed having a captive audience, I also really wanted them to catch Lennie.

I leaned over far enough so that I could see the wall of windows. It was still white with blowing snow outside, making it difficult to see if Lennie was close or even anywhere in sight, although the wind had died down a little bit.

"What are you guys going to do?" I asked. I didn't like feeling like a sitting duck.

Max took a deep breath and the other officers looked to him for a decision. After a moment, he came up with a plan.

"I think the three of you will come with me," Max said. "We are going to walk a line towards the trees and see if we can find Lennie out there. We will walk slow, guns ready and if we see Lennie, we will try to take him unharmed. Philip will stay here with Tessa until the ambulance arrives."

"What if you don't find Lennie?" I asked.

"Let's just hope that we do," Max said. His calm, steady voice helped soothe me a little. He seemed so in control and sure of what he was doing. "Men, let's go."

The other three officers stood up and moved towards the back door. Max slid closer to me and took my hands in his. He looked me straight in the eye.

"Tessa, I will find him and I will catch him," Max said. "I won't let him hurt you."

He leaned down and gave me a long kiss that I wish could have lasted even longer. But for someone who hated to show public affection, it was long enough.

"Philip, you didn't see anything," Max said. Philip nodded, his eyes still wide as Max stood up to walk to the back door.

Once Max joined the other officers, they all put their heads together and seemed to be formulating a plan together. They each drew their weapon and after a moment, they threw the back door open and disappeared into the blowing snow.

Max was the last one out and before he disappeared, he turned and gave me a quick wink and a smile. While I might be feeling nervous, Max was in his element. I suddenly felt much safer, which was saying a lot considering the Nervous Nellie I was being left with.

I turned and looked at Philip, who seemed so nervous he might have been vibrating. Now all we could do was sit and wait.

•Chapter Thirty-Eight•

As we waited, I wondered if I should try to strike up a conversation but distracting Philip seemed like a bad idea. If Lennie came in, I wanted Philip to be somewhat ready to help.

Instead we sat in silence, both peeking around the edge of the kitchenette's island to try and spot anything we could outside, but all we could see was blowing snow. Philip and I seemed to sit there for ages and I wished I had glanced at a clock or something to know how long we had been like that. It could have been five minutes or five hours; I really had no sense of time.

"Have you heard anything from them Philip?" I asked. I knew he hadn't, but I just needed to break the silence.

"Not yet, ma'am," he said, making me feel ancient. But asking him must have helped because suddenly he seemed ever so slightly more competent.

I nodded, not sure what to do next. The water in the bowl for my feet was getting colder and I knew that if the ambulance didn't come soon we would have to change it to warmer water again. I would give it a few more minutes before I asked Philip for help because if he was helping me get water, he wasn't helping me look out for Lennie. I hoped I wouldn't have to choose between my frostbitten feet and my life.

"Did you hear that?" Philip said.

I scrunched my face up and listened hard, but the only thing I heard was the wind howling outside.

"No, I don't hear anything," I said.

"There it is again," Philip cried. "It's like a banging. Do you think it is Lennie?"

I still couldn't hear anything. I was starting to think that Philip's nerves were making him hear things when suddenly, I heard it too. My eyes grew wide as I realized there was a banging on the back door.

"What should we do?" Philip asked. If I hadn't been so nervous, I would have laughed at how ridiculous this was. The police officer assigned to protect me was asking me for advice. I supposed I should tell him what I thought.

"Well, it could be Lennie or it could be Max," I said. "So I'm not sure what we should do. You are the officer here. It is up to you if you think you should go check the door or not."

Philip nodded as he mulled it over. I could see him weighing it back and forth in his mind. If he opened it and it was Lennie, he would have to face down a killer by himself. If it was Max, he would have backup. If he didn't open it and it was Lennie, Lennie might escape or run somewhere else to cause more trouble. If he didn't open it and it was Max, he could get in trouble. It really was a situation where he probably wouldn't win, no matter what he opted to do.

"I'm going to open the door," he said. He took out his baton and handed it to me. "Just in case anything should happen, I'll give you this to protect yourself."

I don't think a baton would help much if Lennie came at me with his gun, but I appreciated the gesture. It was better than having nothing.

Philip drew his gun and took a deep breath. I looked him in the eyes and gave him a solemn nod, which seemed to bolster his confidence. His chest puffed out and he seemed to grow six inches in that moment. He nodded back before he slid out from behind the counter.

As he slowly walked towards the back door, I slid so that I could just see him and the back door. I wanted to be as hidden as possible, just in case. The bowl of water was now only lukewarm, room temperature. Maybe I should have asked Philip to change it before he left. But I hadn't thought he would be leaving, so now I was stuck with it.

Another bang came from the back door and I wish the door had some sort of window. Of course in this situation where it would come in so handy, it was simply a solid door. I supposed if there was a window and it was Lennie, it would have only been worse because he could have shot through it.

Philip had one hand on the door knob and the other holding his gun. I could see his mouth moving and even though I was terrible at reading lips, I could see he was counting. When he got to three, he pulled down the handle and pushed it open just enough that it wasn't latched anymore.

He kicked the door open into the blowing snow and lunged out, both hands holding his gun. The only thing out there was snow, a lot of blowing snow. It was starting to pick up again and it was getting even harder to see. I hoped that Max and the other officers were safe. I wasn't sure how long they had been gone, but it seemed like quite a while.

Philip stood in the doorway, his gun pointed out. I could see his entire body heaving with adrenaline and I suddenly realized my heart was almost beating out of my chest.

"I don't see anything," Philip said finally.

"I don't either," I confirmed from my place behind the counter. Had we just been hearing things because of our nerves?

After another moment of standing at attention, staring out into the snow, Philip turned and looked at me. He shrugged and I shrugged back. He had tried and there wasn't much else he could have done.

Suddenly, an arm appeared from the outside of

the door, holding a large, thick stick. I inhaled sharply before I managed to find my voice.

"Philip, look out!" I screamed.

Philip whirled around, but before he could do anything, the stick came down hard on his head. Philip crumpled into a pile on the floor, halfway inside the park building and halfway outside in the swirling snow.

Lennie appeared in the doorway, stepping over Philip's limp boy and I quickly scooted back behind the kitchenette counter. In the brief glance I got of him I didn't see a gun, but I did see the large stick he had used to hit Philip. He knew I was in here because I was sure he had heard me scream for Philip. Even though he may have ditched the gun, he was still much more mobile than I was with my frostbitten feet.

I took a breath and decided I needed to ditch the water. I grabbed one of the cupboard doors next to me and slowly opened it. It was empty and big enough that I could just barely fit. I needed to hide because sooner or later he would come into the kitchenette. There weren't that many places to hide in the park building.

As soon as I was in, I shut the cupboard door and tried to quiet my breathing. My heart seemed to be pounding a million beats per minute and felt like it would jump up and out of my throat at any time. My hands were starting to shake from the adrenaline, but thinking of my hands gave me an idea.

I was still worried about my feet, so I needed to do something to help. I took my big, thick mittens off of my hands and shoved them onto my feet. They should help keep my feet somewhat warm even if I felt like I had big penguin flippers now.

"Tessa, I know you're in here somewhere," I heard Lennie call. "There aren't that many hiding places. I'll find you soon enough."

I focused all of my attention on breathing quietly and steadily while I sat in the dark. Would Max be able to come back and help me in time?

•Chapter Thirty-Nine•

I closed my eyes and focused on listening to Lennie's footsteps. He seemed to be on the other side of the room, over by the fireplace. If I was lucky, he would take a long time making his way across the room and by then Max would be back with the other officers.

But then a horrible thought entered my mind. Maybe Lennie had already attacked Max and the other officers. Maybe the reason I hadn't seen a gun was that he'd used all of his bullets to shoot them, so he abandoned it. Maybe my only hope was me.

Tears sprung to my eyes as I thought about the police officers out in the snow, needing help. I thought about Philip, unconscious in the doorway. I thought about Max and what I would do if he died. Tears instantly sprung to my eyes, but I pushed them away with my hand. I needed to concentrate. If anyone was hurt out there, I needed to get help to them because I was their only hope now.

Lennie's footsteps were getting closer. I assumed he was checking under all of the tables and chairs in the room. There were a lot of them, so it was taking him a good amount of time to do it, which meant I could hopefully come up with some sort of plan.

… Winter Festival Murder

I tried to think, but nothing was springing to mind. I had used all of my brain power on my last escape plan. The only weapon I had was the baton Philip left with me but seeing as I could hardly stand up, it wouldn't be much use from a kneeling position. The cupboard was empty, so there was nothing else I could use. I wasn't going to give up hope, but I started to think it may be the end of the line for me.

Suddenly, the cupboard door slammed open and Lennie was standing in front of me, bending down to look inside the cabinet. His eyes were still wild and his teeth were clenched in a maniacal grin.

"Ah ha," he yelled. "I told you that you wouldn't be able to hide from me."

Lennie reached inside and tried to grab me by the coat, but I pushed as far back from him as I could. The cupboard I was in had a door on the other side and I ended up falling backwards out into the large room. I needed to get up and moving. I grabbed a chair and pulled myself up, trying to ignore the pain coming from my feet. The mittens were helping a little, but walking certainly wasn't helping them.

I grasped my baton and held it up as Lennie walked around the kitchenette island holding the stick he had used to knock Philip out. I backed up as he walked, hoping to keep as much distance between us as possible.

"What happened to your gun Lennie?" I asked.

Winter Festival Murder

"You only have a stick now?"

"I dropped the gun somewhere in the snow," he said. "But it doesn't matter. You saw what I can do with it. That boy officer didn't stand a chance against it and neither will you."

"But why are you still coming after me?" I asked. "Do you really think you're going to escape now?"

Lennie's face was contorted in anger. He was sneering at me and his eyes were wild. His cheeks were red and white from being out in the cold, blowing wind and his hair was sticking up all over from wearing a hat he had apparently lost along the way.

"You're the only thing standing in my way," Lennie said. "And you were the one that threw away the medallion I worked so hard for."

Through the anger, Lennie's sadness started to seep in. Tears started to run down his ice-cold cheeks. He was focused solely on me and killing me because I had been the one to get rid of the medallion.

"I've worked all my life to be the best and I always manage to come in second place, never first," he said. "Here I'd finally done it. I had found the medallion and even though I'd had to shoot that pathetic Gerald, I had gotten away with it until you figured it out. For once, I just want to be the one who wins."

Winter Festival Murder

    I could feel the warmth of the fireplace on the back of my legs and I glanced back, realizing I was almost out of space. There was nowhere else to go from here and my feet were killing me.
    Over Lennie's shoulder, I could see some movement, but I didn't dare look. I was afraid that if I did, he would think I was trying to trick him again and that would not go over well. I just hoped that whatever or whoever I could see moving would help me out.

•Chapter Forty•

I looked around but even if I had working feet, there was no real way to escape. In front of me was Lennie brandishing the large stick he had brought in. Behind me was a large stone fireplace complete with raging fire. On either side of me were round tables with chairs all around. If I tried to go either way, I'd have to jump and slide over the table like I was a character in an old sitcom sliding across the hood of a car. My nonathletic body wouldn't be able to handle that even if I hadn't gotten frostbite on my feet.

"Are there any last words you'd like to say?" Lennie said, raising the stick over his head as he walked closer and closer to me. A glint of something metallic sticking out of one of his pockets caught my eye and I realized he had grabbed a large knife from the kitchenette. For a man who never was the best, he was doing a great job of being scary.

"Yes, I'd just like to say one thing," I said. "I think you are only making things worse for yourself. This all started with something that you did in self defense. Sure, the police may have doubted that if you told them, but if you had reported it I'm sure the truth would have come out."

Lennie snorted, his mouth turned up into a grimace. I could see some movement between some of the tables, but whoever was coming this way was crouched down too low for me to see them. I didn't really care who it was that was coming to my rescue; I just knew I needed help. Hope started to bubble up inside of me.

"Now you've made things so much worse," I continued. If I could drag this spiel on long enough, then whoever was currently creeping this way could get here before Lennie smashed my head in. "Now you've added attempted murder, assaulting a police officer, and who knows what else. Everyone knows it was you. Do you really think you'll be able to get out of this and then what? Just run your entire life to stay one step ahead of the police?"

Lennie's face fell slightly. He had been so focused on the medallion and keeping it safe that he hadn't thought more than one step ahead. I could almost see it all flashing before his eyes. The wild light in his eyes slowly dimmed as the realization settled in that he hadn't finally become the winner he had wanted to be his entire life. He had only managed to ruin his own life, along with Gerald's.

"Did you even find the medallion out there?" I asked gently. I needed to keep talking, but I wasn't sure what else to say that wouldn't anger him.

"No," he admitted.

Lennie slowly lowered the stick down by his side. He stared at the floor just in front of me.

Philip's red hair appeared above the table just behind Lennie to the right. I managed to blink at him to acknowledge that I saw him, but I didn't want to give him away. Philip's face looked cool and collected, nothing like the nervous boy who had been assigned to guard me earlier. Maybe the knock on the head had knocked some maturity into him.

"I didn't even find the medallion," Lennie said softly. His entire world was crashing down around him.

"Put the stick down, Lennie," Philip said. He popped out of his hiding spot and pointed his gun at Lennie.

Lennie's head snapped up and the fire was back in his eyes. Before he could do anything, I leapt toward him, grabbing onto him like a baby monkey. Lennie stumbled backward, falling down onto his back on the ground. I kept my grip on him, only loosening up when he was fully on the ground.

I grabbed the stick and ripped it out of his hands while Philip jumped on top of him also. I grabbed the knife out of his pocket and tossed it aside. Philip and I looked at each other for a moment, both wondering what to do next when we heard the back door open.

Max's head popped in and when he saw Philip and I sitting on top of Lennie, his eyes grew wide. He threw the door open and ran in, zig-zagging through the tables to help us with the other three officers following close behind.

The other three officers descended on Lennie to help Philip handcuff him as Max lifted me up and off of Lennie. He held me close in his arms and I wrapped my arms around his neck. As I snuggled my face into the rough stubble on his neck, I could feel tears falling down my face. I wasn't sad or upset, but all of the emotions of the day came pouring out of me.

"Let's get you out to the ambulance," Max said.

I looked up and could just barely make out the red and blue flashing lights pulling up through the blowing snow. Max carried me to the front door before he turned and called out to the other officers.

"Philip, I know I told you to stay with Tessa, but let's swap roles just this once," Max said.

"Yes sir," Philip said. His chest was puffed out with pride as the other officers were taking turns congratulating him and slapping him on the back. At least something good had come out of this.

Max ran out just as the paramedics were climbing out of the rig. They opened the doors in back and Max climbed right inside with me still in his arms. I had almost forgot about how much my feet hurt until we were in the ambulance slowly making our way to the hospital.

"Sorry it took us so long," the EMT in the passenger seat called back to us. "It is blowing so hard we almost ran off the road a few times. We are just lucky to be here in one piece."

"That's alright," I said. "This way Max gets to be the one to take me to the hospital."

Max wrapped me in a tight hug once more before he slid me over to lay on the stretcher. I knew that he worked closely with all sorts of first responders, so I didn't blame him for not wanting to be mushy-gushy around them.

But he did hold my hand the entire time we slid to the hospital in the ambulance.

•Chapter Forty-One•

The doctors at the hospital assured me that my case of frostbite was mild, but they encouraged me to stay for a while so that they could warm up my feet and make sure there was no other damage to them. I laid in the hospital bed, watching some old game show from decades before I was born, hoping my family would listen to my plea for them to not come to the hospital. When I contacted them, I told them that I needed two things: someone to go get my car from the parking lot of the park and someone else to ready the couch for me to recover, complete with a pepperoni pizza from Mike's. So far, they seemed to be listening.

The curtain around my hospital bed parted and Max came back in with a big smile on his face. He had stepped out for a moment to catch up on what had happened once we left for the hospital.

"Is it safe to say that Lennie did not somehow slip out of police custody after we left?" I asked.

"Nope, he is down at the jail right now," Max said. "And he is singing like a canary."

I threw my head back and laughed as Max smiled his big, dumb smile. Max always knew just what to say to send me into hysterics. It was one of the things that made me fall in love with him in high school and it was something that still made me love him today.

"Isn't that what they say when someone rats out their partners in crime?" I asked. "I'm pretty sure Lennie was working alone."

"You're right, I guess," Max said. "But he is spilling his guts about everything from Gerald's death to how he planned today."

Max strolled over and sat back down in the uncomfortable looking chair that was next to my hospital bed where he had stationed himself two hours ago when we first got here. I put my hand out towards him and he immediately took it in his and gave it a squeeze.

"So that Loony Bin keychain and the footprints in the trees were Lennie's, were they?" I asked.

"Actually, it sounds like those must have been Gerald's," Max said. "We think Gerald snuck down the sidewalk and through the trees before he attacked Lennie. Lennie said he was never back in the trees."

"Well, what about the bank paper in the parking lot?" I asked. Surely that had to be tied to him if the other clues weren't.

"That was Lennie's," Max said. "Apparently he was not doing as well in his seed business as we all thought. The bank had just sent him that letter a few days before the medallion hunt started. It seems that he not only wanted to win the medallion, but he thought the prize money might be helpful."

While I sat there looking at Max, I wondered why I'd been so set on not dating anyone seriously. Of course, I know Max was only looking to date casually, but I wondered how he felt about it now. Maybe he was starting to fall more in love with me just like I was with him.

I was about to open my mouth and ask him when the curtains were shoved violently aside and Mandy came racing into the emergency room bay.

"I know you said no family, but this is how we got around the rule," Mandy said before I could protest. She was right, of course, and was utilizing a loophole I may have realized existed if I hadn't been so busy making goo-goo eyes towards Max. "Hey Max."

"Hey Mandy," Max said, his cheeks getting a little red. "Tessa's doing alright. They said they are going to let her go soon. You can drive her home because I don't have a car. I'll just call the station to send someone to come get me."

Max winked at me before he bent down and gave me a quick squeeze.

"I'll call you later and we can set up a date," he whispered into my ear. "I knew I wouldn't be able to keep you all to myself for too long."

He gave me a quick kiss on the cheek and I felt my cheeks start to blush, just a bit. Max gave one last wave and disappeared through the curtain and into the busy emergency room.

"I hope I didn't interrupt anything important," Mandy said. I leaned over to try and shove her and almost fell out of the bed. Instead of shoving Mandy, I ended up clinging to her arm before she helped lift my center of gravity back up onto the hospital bed.

"No, not really, but it would have been nice if you'd come like ten minutes from now," I grumbled. I would just have to wait until another time to talk to Max about our relationship. At least he didn't seem to be mad at me anymore so I wouldn't have to worry about that.

Mandy grinned at me. I'm sure she could somehow read my mind to know what I was talking about because she was just that good.

"Are your doctors coming back soon?" she asked as she wiggled her eyebrows conspiratorially. Mandy opened her purse a crack and beckoned for me to look inside. "I brought you a little something."

Inside sitting on top of a napkin was a round donut with pink frosting and heart sprinkles. My mouth started to salivate just looking at it.

"I was doing a little practicing for Valentine's Day when I heard what had happened to you," Mandy said with a shrug.

As we waited for the doctor to come back and discharge me, Mandy passed me bites of donut so that we wouldn't get busted by the sudden appearance of a medical professional. Finally, a doctor came by and gave me my papers. A nurse helped wheel me out to Mandy's car, which she pulled around to the door.

I spent the rest of the night reclining on the couch, eating pizza and retelling the story of what had happened with Lennie every time someone new came in to check on how I was doing.

The biggest surprise was when the door opened and Ronald and Chelsea both stepped into my living room. Up until this point, it had been all family and close friends, so I felt a little embarrassed when the mayor and someone who hates me walked in.

"We didn't come together," Chelsea quickly said, answering the first question on everyone's mind. "We just both happened to get here at the same time."

"I just wanted to make sure you were alright," Ronald said. Today's sweater vest was baby blue and I wondered if he had been picking vests that he thought would fit with the Below Zero Festival theme of the week.

"I didn't care, I just want to hear the story," Chelsea said.

I rolled my eyes at her and sent a quick message to Max asking if he wanted me talking to the press, not that I wanted to flatter Chelsea by calling her that. He sent back a quick confirmation that I was allowed to tell her anything and everything.

So I launched into my story one final time, making sure not to skip any of the details. When I got to the part about my frostbite, Chelsea sneered as she glanced down at my bandaged feet.

When I reached the end of the story, everyone sat with their mouths open, under the spell of my totally weird, but captivating story. Chelsea looked like she was actually kind of impressed and even my family who had heard the story multiple times now sat with their attention on me.

"I can't even imagine Tessa," Ronald said. "But thank you for saving the town's medallion hunt. I feel like after catching Lennie, we can safely hold another medallion hunt next year. And I just know the entire town will want to say thank you at the festival farewell party tomorrow."

"What farewell party?" Chelsea and I both asked at the same time.

"Listen to the radio tomorrow morning and I'll give all of the details," Ronald said mysteriously before grabbing his jacket and leaving the living room. I could see him pulling his phone out of his pocket before he left and I knew he was starting to call around to pull together this crazy party that I would have to attend.

For now, my parents saw Chelsea out and

helped me to my bedroom, with a little assistance from Mandy. I would need to rest up if I was expected to attend this new party.

•Chapter Forty-Two•

The next morning, the radio announced that there would be a festival farewell party downtown so that we could end the festival on a good note instead of the attempted murder. Apparently no one had thought about the fact that maybe the girl with frostbite on her feet would want an inside party instead of an outside one, but it was the Below Zero Festival to celebrate being outside in the winter so I sucked it up and told myself I didn't have to stay long.

Mandy had borrowed a wheelchair from somewhere for me to use and after making sure I was suitably bundled up, we headed out. My feet had some boot warmers shoved down by my toes along with some warm socks which seemed to be working for now. I wasn't able to drive because of my feet, but I was shoved unceremoniously into the front seat and driven downtown.

Ronald had actually managed to pull together a somewhat decent party on such short notice. There were some of the local food trucks around, all giving away free food. We made sure to swing by the corn dog stand before they ran out of free corn dogs.

The main street had been shut down and kids were running around playing in the snow. There was also a stage and music was currently blasting out of the loud speakers that were set up on top. I actually had to admit I was a little impressed.

As I was sitting in the wheelchair scarfing down the two corn dogs I had managed to snag, Donna suddenly appeared out of the crowd with Bobby close by. She made a beeline straight for me and practically threw herself into my lap to give me a hug.

"I can't believe what happened," she said. "I'm so glad you are okay. And I wanted to thank you. I feel like my soul can have a little peace now that we know what happened to Gerald."

I nodded, glad something good came out of the situation. Donna still had a smile on her face, though, so I was a little confused until she somehow read my mind and explained.

"I'm extra happy today too," she continued. "I got a promotion and a raise at work, so I don't have to worry about money for a while. Bobby and I are going to do just fine."

"I'm so glad to hear that Donna," I said before she waved goodbye and headed off, tugging Bobby along with her. I really was happy for her, just like anytime something good happened to a good person.

The music that was flowing out of the speakers cut off suddenly and some feedback from the microphone came out instead. I looked over to see

Winter Festival Murder

Ronald sheepishly holding the microphone. Someone must have adjusted something because suddenly the feedback stopped and Ronald started to speak.

"Hello Shady Lakers," he said. He was wearing what seemed like a big, fake, mayoral smile, but really it was just how Ronald always looked. "Welcome to the farewell party and I really appreciate that you all took the time to come to this party on such short notice."

Of course the audience gave a little polite applause like a good Minnesotan audience always does. Ronald grinned and I took the chance to look around the crowd a little bit. It seemed like most of the town had turned out and I was happy to see Clark towards the back of the crowd standing next to Rich and Charlie. Mandy and Trevor were standing not too far away from me. I wasn't sure if Trevor actually looked happy for once or if I just knew he was happy to be with Mandy and so he looked happier than he used to. Either way, I felt like this experience had also brought me a tiny bit closer to Trevor. If nothing else, it helped me not hate him anymore.

"The biggest reason I called all of you here was because there is a townsperson here who needs some special recognition," Ronald was saying.

My stomach dropped when I realized that townsperson was me. I knew he would try something like this, but for some reason, it still blindsided me.

Winter Festival Murder

All I could think about was how I was supposed to get on stage if I was in a wheelchair.

"Tessa, if you could please come up on the, ah, to the, umm," Ronald started to stutter as he looked around, realizing there was no ramp for me to be pushed up. "Oh dear."

"Don't worry Ronald, I'll bring her up."

Max appeared next to me, my knight in shining armor as ever. He bent down and put my one arm around his neck hoisting me up like I weighed nothing. Max might be on the shorter side, but he is built like a bodybuilder.

He walked me up the stairs onto the stage where Ronald was waiting. I felt a little awkward, but Ronald just looked happy that we had figured out a way to get me up on stage.

"Oh good, thank you Officer Marcus," Ronald said before turning back to the crowd. "I'm sure you've all read the newspaper this morning, so I will save you from my replay of the story, but suffice to say that Tessa has saved the medallion hunt and the festival so that it can happen again next year. So this year, I think it's only fair that we show our appreciation by presenting her with this year's medallion."

The crowd clapped and Ronald pulled the medallion out of his pocket, making a big show of holding it up in the air before presenting it to me. I took the medallion from him, not exactly sure what to do with it besides hold it in my hands.

Max thankfully gave a little wave and walked me back down the stairs before it got too awkward. He set me down in the wheelchair and then started to wheel me back towards where Clark was standing next to Rich and Charlie. Clark smiled at me, but seemed kind of distant. I hoped he wasn't too upset about Max carrying me up onto the stage. He shouldn't be; it wasn't like he'd offered to help.

"I'm glad you're okay Tessa," he said before excusing himself. I couldn't help but notice that he was headed right towards where Chelsea was standing in the crowd. I chose to ignore that for now and turned back to Charlie and Rich.

"Tessa, I'm not sure how I can repay you," Charlie said. He bent down and shook my hand. "Not only did you help to get me out of jail, but now my father knows about my money troubles and he's agreed to help me. I feel so stupid like I should have just asked for help at the beginning but at least now everything is falling into place. And you are who I have to thank for it."

"The next time you stop in for dinner at the Loony Bin, it's on us," Rich said. "The next few times, I suppose I should say."

Charlie and Rich excused themselves to get back to work at the bar and Max and I were left together. He wheeled me over and parked me next to a park bench before running to get us two large, warm soft pretzels. And while we watched the snow fall, we ate our pretzels in silence. It felt good to be next to someone I think I was falling in love with again. Maybe, just maybe I was done dating casually. I just hoped that Max felt the same.

•About the Author•

Linnea West lives in Minnesota with her husband and two children. She taught herself to read at the age of four and published her first poem in a local newspaper at the age of seven. After a turn as a writer for her high school newspaper, she went to school for English Education and Elementary Education. She didn't start writing fiction until she was a full time working mother. Besides reading and writing, she spends her time chasing after her children, watching movies with her husband, and doing puzzle books. Learn more about her and her upcoming books by visiting her website and signing up for her newsletter at linneawestbooks.com.

Note From the Author: Reviews are gold to authors! If you've enjoyed this book, would you consider rating it and reviewing it on Amazon? Thank you!

•Other Books in the Series•

Small Town Minnesota Cozy Mystery Series
Book One-Halloween Hayride Murder
Book Two-Christmas Shop Murder
Book Three-Winter Festival Murder
Book Four-Valentine's Blizzard Murder
Book Five-Spring Break Murder

Made in United States
North Haven, CT
21 October 2022